Rasta Love

By: Alicea Ellis

ISBN 978-976-654-056-2

RASTA LOVE

Publisher: Irie Books Ja

Copyright © 2019 by Alicea L. Ellis

For more information:

author@iriebooksja.com

www.iriebooksja.com

Please Enjoy…

Dear Reader,

I wish to thank you for sharing in this grand experience. My first Romance novel 'Rasta Love' is now a reality.

I have taken my time in carving this beautiful, romance for your reading pleasure, as I believe we all have so much love to give and true romance can never be outdated.

This book was influenced by the knowledge I have gained from studying history and seeing the struggles faced by Rastafarians, from basic survival to finding true love, as they were never truly accepted by society. I therefore dedicate this piece to all true Rastafarians.

I pray my work will be both enlightening and fulfilling.

Thank you

Rasta Love

The Elizabeth Blackwood story

Chapter One

"Elizabeth," her mom bellowed.

"Coming mom," was all Liz could say before running off in the direction of home. She didn't even get a chance to say goodbye to her friend Tafari.

"How many times am I going to tell you not to play with that Rasta boy next door?"

"But mom, he's my friend" she replied more defensively than intended.

"No, he's not your friend. He is the son of the help. Why can't his father take him to the barber?"

Elizabeth smiled. "Mom, it's only a style, his hair looks fine."

"Don't talk back to me little girl. As a matter-of-fact, go to your room."

Elizabeth walked off and waited until she was out of her mother's view to smile and place her hand to her heart. She really liked Tafari Messiah and nothing her mom said would change that.

While in her room, Elizabeth took the opportunity to watch Tafari through her bedroom window. He was so helpful. Currently, he was helping his mother to fetch water. At the tender age of fourteen, he was the perfect gentleman.

He was also very good with his hands. He could build just about anything. He even built a whole tree house all by himself. It was her desire to see what the inside looked like, but her mom kept such close watch on her she could only look at it through her window and imagine.

After carrying water for his mom, he spent the remainder of the afternoon building what looked like a chair. She watched him keenly and observed how precise he was at taking measurements, and how well he handled his tools. He was wearing khakis that were too short for school. He was barefooted with his hair hanging loosely on his shoulder and all the time he was smiling and nodding his head. She couldn't hear the music, but she could see he was having fun.

They were from different worlds, Elizabeth was the rich man's daughter. Her father, Stan Blackwood owned hectares of land in their community with at least twenty men working the fields and tending to animals daily. The Blackwood name carried much precedence on the south coast of Jamaica where they lived. Her dad was one of the richest planters' this side of the island.

Her mom, Loviet Blackwood, a teacher by profession, no longer worked after becoming a mom. There was no need to work as she was well kept with maids at her service. Elizabeth was sent to the best school around, roughly six miles from home.

Her parents wanted her to be a doctor, she wanted to be a dancer. Her mom however was not fond of that idea as she said dancing was for uneducated people who had nothing better to do with their lives. Her dad went along with everything her mom said so he had already started looking at schools where she could study medicine as soon as she graduated high school.

Tafari, on the other hand, was the son of Marcus Messiah, a skilled farm hand, and Lucille Messiah who was a maid in the house. Today being Sunday, they didn't have to work. When she asked Tafari what he wanted to become, he said his dream was to be an entertainer. Dancing, singing and playing musical instruments was his passion. He was already so good at them all. He was always playing the drums and even built guitars from wood and strings. He would often play and sing along, pretending he was performing for a crowd. She prayed he would be successful. His mom always had high praises for him, as she always boasted on how well he was doing in school and that he could be anything he wanted to be. She had other children but he was dearest to her, as he was her last child and only boy. Elizabeth knew his mom would support his dreams, whatever he wanted to be. Elizabeth wished her mom would be more like Aunt Lucy, as she was affectionately called.

Elizabeth heard her mom's call and realized it was time for dinner. She looked on a little longer, capturing his essence so she could feed on it while at dinner with her parents. They spoke about the same things every Sunday afternoon, what was new in the news, Liz's performance at school, and the plans they had for the week. She always sits there and listens, bored out of her mind.
Just before walking away, she touched the window as if to say, see you later my love. If only you knew how I feel about you. She was only fourteen but she knew this feeling was love.

Chapter Two

The next morning, Elizabeth was up and ready for school before her driver could arrive. She had a fine breakfast Aunt Lucy had prepared; fried eggs with ripe plantain and a slice of toast. She even made oatmeal porridge in addition to that.

Uncle John, her driver came about seven to take her to school. As she exited the gate she saw Tafari. He was also on his way to school. He attended a school that was within walking distance from home, while she went to an all girls' school several communities away.

"Good morning Tafari," she called with a smile.

He barely turned his head and said, "good morning." She stared after him as he walked up the street, and as if he realized he had not done well enough, he turned around with a brilliant, white teeth smile, "have a great day at school Liz," then walked away.

She was blushing so badly her cheeks burned. She noticed Uncle John, her first and only driver and dear friend to her dad watching her through his rear-view mirror but that didn't affect her mood. This was going to be an awesome day.

"I see you have a crush," she heard Uncle John's voice pierce through her thoughts.

"Why would you think that Uncle John?" Liz asked innocently.

He shrugged a little before answering "It could be because I have known you since you were a baby and I have never seen you smile the way you did when you saw that Rasta boy this morning." She knew he was teasing.

"His name is Tafari," she snapped "and no he's not my crush, he's my friend."

"Ok, ok, Tafari," he smiled widely.

Nothing else was said between the two until they arrived at her school. As she exited and walked towards the gate he called after her, "have a great day at school Liz," mocking Tafari's earlier words before driving off.

Liz had Religious Education first period, it was a subject she didn't particularly enjoy. She sat there staring at the board, not seeing anything.

"When you finally come back to us Ms. Blackwood, would you like to share with the class what all that daydreaming was about?"

Liz looked up at her teacher towering above her and smiled. "I'm back. Trust me, there is nothing to share that would be more entertaining than your teaching Miss Spencer. You are the best."

The tension in her teacher's face slowly eased. "Interesting artwork," she remarked looking at the notebook on Liz's desk.

Liz looked down to see what the teacher was talking about and that's when she realized she had been doodling little hearts on her page. "Oh that, that's nothing miss," she said as innocently as she could.

"Come see me after class, I have a note to send to your parents."

"Okay Miss," Liz answered hanging her head. She couldn't help feeling panicked in the pit of her stomach.

What kind of note was Miss Spencer going to send? Was she going to tell her parents she was daydreaming and making hearts? She didn't want her mother to get any ideas. She was already way too overprotective.

As difficult as it was to handle, Liz understood why her mother was like that, she had been trying for years to get pregnant and after multiple doctor visits and medication that didn't help, she had given up on the idea of ever becoming a mother, so when she finally had Liz, she did everything to protect her little miracle.

She sat there nervously paying attention for the remainder of the class. When teaching was over, she had to muster all her courage to get up and go to her teacher's desk.

To her surprise, Mrs. Spencer handed her a note with a permission slip attached for her parents to sign giving her consent to represent the school at a cultural exposition happening in Kingston in a month.

She expressed how she had enjoyed the performance Liz had given earlier that month at the school's prayer breakfast. She told Liz there would be practice in the evenings leading up to the event, and that it was detailed in the note.

This made Elizabeth very excited, she loved dancing and the thought of doing so in front of an audience really got her blood pumping. "Yes miss, I will have it signed, and I'll take it to you early in the morning."

 Miss Spencer smiled. Elizabeth reminded her so much of herself when she was younger, she had such a passion for reciting poems and that blossomed into her becoming a passionate teacher and president of the school's dance and drama club. She had danced at Jamaica's Independence

Celebration in 1962, now here she was twenty years later preparing her own students to take part. This made her super excited as she really enjoyed framing young minds.

Elizabeth bid her teacher goodbye and headed for the door. "And Liz," she paused to give Elizabeth the chance to turn around, "boys will be around after you have finished studying, trust me, you are not ready for the pain that can come from a broken heart."

Liz thought about it for a minute before answering with a sigh, "Ok miss."

She met up with her friend Dianne who was waiting outside. "So girl, are you in trouble? Did teacher write a note to inform your parents that you were busy writing love letter and not paying attention in her class?"

"First of all, I was not writing a love letter, and second, she wants me to dance in Kingston in a few weeks," Liz answered with much attitude.

"Wow, that's awesome girl. I'm so proud of you." Dianne knew how much her friend loved to dance. "Now let's go have some lunch and talk about that cute Rasta guy next door." They laughed and held hands heading to the cafeteria.

Elizabeth could not wait to share her excitement with her parents as they sat down to dinner that evening. She said grace and then announced, "Mom, Dad I have great news!"

"What could be so important that it couldn't wait until after dinner Elizabeth, did your manners fly out the door?" Dad paused as if waiting for an answer before continuing, "You know we eat first and after the table is cleared, then we talk."

Loviet knew it wasn't like her daughter to interrupt dinner, so it must have been something that couldn't wait. "Elizabeth honey, we know you are aware it's not acceptable to interrupt dinner for any reason, but seeing you're so excited, I'll give you a pass."

"Thanks Mom, sorry dad, but I am about to burst from excitement. I have been asked to represent my school dancing at a National event in Kingston in a month."

Mom knew how much Elizabeth loved to dance. She even allowed her to join the dance club at school. "This is really exciting news baby. What piece will you be performing?"

"Do you remember that piece I performed at the prayer breakfast last month? That's the one Miss Spencer asked me to do."

"Oh wow, I really enjoyed that performance." Dad shook his head in agreement.

"I have a permission slip for you to sign."

"Ok honey, after dinner I sure will."

Chapter Three

Elizabeth was dying to share her exciting news with Tafari. The next day at school she eagerly anticipated the end of classes so she could get home. Today was the day that mom did errands in town so that would give her at least an hour to go next door and chat with him.

Thankfully practise wasn't until tomorrow evening. That evening when Uncle John came she was already waiting at the school gate. He would normally be there for at least ten minutes before she came running, but not today.

"Good evening Liz, You seem very eager to get home this evening. He pulled away from the curb. Your mom told me you will be performing at the annual festival held in Kingston, you must be very excited."

"I am elated Uncle John."

"So, should I assume that your eagerness to get home is to practise in front of your mirror, or, are you using the opportunity to talk with that boy that lives next door? Tafari, I believe you said his name was? I know you really like him Lizzie."

Elizabeth blushed heavily. "I do like him Uncle John, but how did you figure it out?"

"Unmm," he hesitated as if searching for the explanation. "Maybe because I have two teenage daughters", he laughed, "plus I've known you since you were just a baby. I see the way your eyes shine whenever he says hello in the mornings."

"You're not going to tell my parents, are you, Uncle John?"

"Oh no honey, I wouldn't risk losing that glow in your eyes. Once it remains innocent." He looked at her through the rear view mirror, "It is innocent, right Elizabeth?"
"It is, Uncle John, I promise. I would never do anything to jeopardize my future."
"That's my girl," John said shaking his head, "I am really happy to hear you say that Lizzie."
"I hope you and the girls will be at the festival to support me, Uncle John."
"We wouldn't miss it for the world baby girl." He fancied Liz one of his girls as she had grown closely with his two girls, being born the same year as his first.
When Uncle John dropped her off at the gate, he called after her before she could run off, "Now Liz, remember, your mom will be home in an hour or less. I am going to get her now from the hair salon."
"Ok, thanks Uncle John." With that she disappeared up the path.
Liz hurriedly changed from her uniforms and headed through the back door before Aunt Lucy could see her and inquire about her homework.
She was next door calling Tafari within a minute. He was in his tree house as usual. That's where he spent most of his evenings. She always wondered what it is he did for entertainment up there, and she was determined to find out, just not today.
"Yes Elizabeth," his calm, quiet voice resounded like music in her ear.
She watched as he came down the ladder he used as steps. She found herself wondering, "could he really be my forever?" Her heart skipped a few beats as he walked

towards her. "If you only know how I feel about you, Prince Tafari," she added to the conversation she was having with herself.

"To what do I owe this pleasure," he asked smiling.

Liz stood there staring at him, fighting to find her words. When she finally did, she asked, "You know of that grand festival that is held in Kingston every year?"

"Yes, I have heard of it."

"I will be performing there this year." Her face gleamed with pride.

Tafari looked at her enjoying the melody in her voice and the sparkle in her eyes, before responding, "Wow, that's great Liz, I know you will give a show stopping performance. You're so good at everything you do."

Liz hung her head as she didn't want him to see how badly she blushed.

He wanted to hug her so badly but he wasn't going to risk being caught by her parents and getting her into trouble." In time," he said silently to his eager hands.

"So what song will you be dancing to?"

"Oh a combination of songs from Toots and The Maytels, Bob Marley, The Skatalytes and more."

"Oh, yea," Tafari looked at her wide-eyed, "what do you know about that?"

Laughing out loudly, she replied, "I learned from you. I always hear you listening to them on your stereo, so I asked your mom and she told me their names. I love reggae music," she said swaying her hips before realizing.

"Ok then, well I am glad I was able to inspire you,"

"You did," She could feel her cheeks burn again. When she recovered, she asked, "So when are you going to give me a tour of your tree house?"

"Tour?" Tafari asked amused. "It's nothing in comparison to that palace you live in. I'm sure you wouldn't be fascinated."

"I am fascinated by everything you do."

The words were out before she could check them. She fell silent, staring at him, staring back at her, wishing the ground would open and swallow her, to save her from her shame.

She felt his face coming closer but made no effort to stop him. Just as their lips were about to meet, she heard the resounding call like a bell, "Elizabeth!"

"Oh no, mom's home, gotta go," was all she could mumble before running off in the direction of home.

At the door, she could hear her mom talking to herself. "I bet that girl has not even done her assignments. I really should cancel her permission for that damn festival. I've told that girl multiple times to leave the company of that Rasta boy, nothing good can come of it, nothing."

Elizabeth slowly pushed the door, "I'm sorry mom, I promise not to go next door again, please, do not cancel my permission, please mom."

"Ok, stop begging, but one more trip across that fence and you're grounded. You can kiss that damn festival goodbye. Do we have an understanding?"

"Yes, mother."

"Now go and get your assignments done."

Elizabeth walked off to her room with mixed feelings. She wanted to be able to talk with Tafari, but she couldn't risk being withdrawn from her dance. A few days without his company would not kill her and after all, it would be worthwhile, she thought.

Chapter Four

Today was the big day. She had done one month practice and she had her routine down to the tee. There was only one thing that would be missing from her performance, Tafari wouldn't be there to see it.

That thought brought sadness to Elizabeth, but she had to shrug it off. She needed to do great out there. She needed to make her teacher, her parents and all her other supporters proud. She was going to "break a leg" as was popularly said before a theatre performance. The band was on stage setting up, she had heard from another contestant that the band was from a rural school. She wondered how good they were.

She peered through the curtains into the crowd seeking to identify where her parents, Uncle John and the girls, and her support group from school were seated. They were easily identified with the Blue and White attire, the colors that represented her school.

The band started playing, they were so good. They played selections from Bob Marley and some other great artist she could not identify by name, however, it was the kind of music Tafari loved to listen. At least the music would allow her to feel his presence, she thought with a smile.

She watched the first two performers through the curtain, they did well, but she had no doubt she would be better. She was up next, the announcer called her name, she heard the uproar of her support group as she stepped out. She gave a wave to the crowd, then looked around on stage as a way of greeting the MC and musicians.

She froze as she saw Tafari sitting behind the drum sets. She couldn't hide her surprise which quickly turned into excitement. Tafari was here, he would see her performance. He must have known he would be playing here but wanted to surprise her, and what a pleasant surprise it was indeed. Her wish had come through. Now, everything would be perfect. Her song started, and that jolted into action.

She stepped forward with the grace of a swan and started to dance, all the while smiling and enjoying herself. When her routine had ended, she gave a bow as the entire auditorium gave a standing ovation and rounds of applaud. She blew kisses at all and before leaving the stage.
Performances continued, but her knees were too weak to watch. She was also very nervous. She held on to her lucky locket given to her by her grandmother before she passed. "I hope I won," she whispered.
"You did well out there." His words broke in through the silence. She didn't even realize the performances were over.
"Thank you Tafari," she said looking up. "You did mighty fine yourself."
He looked down at his feet, finding it difficult to keep eye contact. He couldn't understand the effect this girl had on him. The sound of her voice always made him melt on the inside.
She got up, placed her arms around his neck with the intention to pull him in for a hug, instead Tafari took her chin in his hands and gave her a sweet, gentle kiss.
She was stunned. Her first kiss from the man of her dreams. Today was perfect.

"And our first place winner is, Elizabeth Blackwood." Those words by the announcer broke through their kiss, bringing them back to reality in a rush.

"You won Liz," Tafari echoed the presenter's announcement.

"I won, I won," she jumped while making her way excitedly to the stage.

She received a bouquet of flowers and a gold medal with lots of cheers and whistles from the crowd.

She gave her vote of thanks to her teacher, Mrs. Spencer, her parents and to all who inspired her to get there. She was unable to say Tafari's name as she didn't wish to upset her mom, but she felt he knew a special thank you was there for him.

Back home, her mother had asked Aunt Lucy to organize a small celebratory party for her. Even the farm workers were invited. They had cake, ice cream, fried chicken, and Tafari. All her favourite things in one place, Liz thought resting her head against a tree in the yard.

"Penny for your thoughts," Tafari came up from behind and whispered in her ear.

She felt her knees go weak beneath her, and it took all she had not to fall.

She turned around with great confidence, "I was just thinking how much I want to dance with you."

He matched her laughter, amused by her boldness. "Then what are we waiting for? Let's dance."

They danced for a long time to some real authentic reggae music, rhythm and blues and rock steady.

Her mom looked on but made no effort to interrupt. Elizabeth wondered if her mom was keeping up appearances, or if she had come to accept Tafari as a friend and potential boyfriend to her. Either way, she wasn't going to question it, she would enjoy it while it lasted.

When the night was over, her mom pulled her close and expressed how proud she had made them. She explained the reason she had not interrupted the dance with Tafari was that, he had done very well today and she believed he deserved to celebrate, not because she accepted their friendship.

"Please know that I forbid any relationship with that boy Elizabeth." She held on to Elizabeth's hand so she could look her directly in the eyes, "I promise you, if you choose to go any further with that Rasta boy, I will disband you as my child, and you will not inherit one iota from your father's estate. Are we clear?"

Her words burned like a fire in the pit of Elizabeth's stomach. How could she agree to this? How could she ever live without Tafari?

Her emotions were a whirlwind of confusion, she wanted to scream, cry, and break something that was of value to her mom, anything that would make her realize how badly she was hurting. How could she want to kill a love so pure?

She pulled away from her mom and without uttering a word, she ran to her room, slammed the door behind her and cried herself to sleep. Her perfect day had not ended so perfect after all.

Chapter Five

Uncle John decided to take the girls out for Ice-cream and cake to celebrate Lizzie's accomplishment at the festival, combined with the celebration of her fifteenth birthday, which was a few days away. His two daughters Adrene and Alex were there. Adrene was the same age as Liz but went to another school in the community.

Alex was a year younger. From time to time Uncle John would take them out on picnics when his wife was around. Aunt Marlene was now working in the states so Liz saw less of the girls. Uncle John's excuse was that he didn't understand the language they spoke anymore, now that they were teenagers.

Tonight, he decided he had to take Liz to celebrate her very proud achievement. It would be painful listening to their endless babbling about the girls didn't like, who was wearing the wrong color lip gloss and which boy was the cutest in the world, but he would survive.

Last night after the celebration, he had witnessed the argument between Liz and her mom, and had seen the hurt in her eyes as she stormed off to her room. He knew it had something to do with that boy next door as he had seen them dance earlier that night.

He hated seeing her hurt. He valued her happiness and her smile as he had been there from the start. He was the one who drove them home from the hospital when she was born. She was like a daughter to him.

Uncle John and the girls left the estate around six in the evening with a promise to get her home by nine. Loviet was not worried as she knew Liz was in good hands. She trusted John with their lives, as he had been their family driver since she married Stan over eighteen years ago.
The girls had a lot of catching up to do, so they started chatting right away.
Uncle John listened to some music and sang along in his head, in an attempt to tune out the girls. He maintained a moderate driving speed though they had a few miles to go before getting to the nearest town. It had rained earlier in the evening, so he had to be careful as the road was still slippery.
The girls started singing along to the radio as one of their favourite songs was now playing. He quickly caught the fever and decided to sing bass.

They were having so much fun that John didn't realize he was headed directly for a van that had switched lanes trying to avoid a hole in the road. Liz unconsciously grabbed the steering wheel and cried, "Uncle John, look out!" The car swerved vigorously as John took control again and tried to avoid a head-on collision with the van, loaded with people and supplies heading to the Coronation Market. The swerve caused Liz to hang on to his arm and John flashed her arm violently, as he tried desperately to regain control of the car.

The tires failed to grip and their screech combined with the cries for "daddy" was deafening. John could no longer control the direction of the car as it slid across the wet roadway, then finally, it slammed into the side of an oncoming truck.

The seat belt did no justice as Liz's head was flung viciously into the dashboard. The impact was such that all was a daze and then, there was nothing.

Liz woke up to the frantic cries of her mother, and that's when she realized she was in the hospital. She had an enormously headache and she could feel her head was bandaged and her neck was in a brace.

In an attempt to comfort her mom she tried lifting her head, but to no avail, so she whispered, "Mom, I'm ok." She raised her hand and placed it on her mother's arm.

"I should never have let you go out, I should never have let you out of my sight. I could have lost you."

Just then, things started coming back to Liz, the screams, the lights, the bang. Fearing the worst Liz asked, "Mom, where are the girls and Uncle John?"

"John suffered a broken wrist and the girls got some minor cuts due to broken glass, but they will all be ok. I'm just so happy you're awake". Her eyes welled up again with tears.

She rubbed her daughters' head, "The doctors said you hit your head pretty hard and would likely be in a coma for days. They are still running some test to determine the extent of your injuries." Stan had gone down to the chapel to pray. Loviet was amazed her husband's prayers had been answered so quickly as their baby who was expected to be in a coma, was awake. She was asking all the right questions too, proving that there was no permanent brain damage. Loviet sighed with relief. She kissed her daughter's forehead, "Get some rest sweetheart. We will be here when you get up in the morning."

A nurse came in shortly after and asked her to step out as she was going to give Liz something to ease the headache so she could sleep soundly throughout the night. Loviet kissed her daughter's cheek again and left the room. She decided to walk down to the chapel to tell her husband the good news.

Aunt Lucy, who was still at the great house when news came of the accident, had shared the horrid news with Tafari when she got home. He had not slept a wink, getting up every few minutes to check for lights in her parents' bedroom, which would indicate that they were back from the hospital.

He planned to wake his mom then so she could get an update. When they returned, it was already past four and mom would be getting up at five so she could be there by six to make breakfast. He decided to wait until then.
As soon as his mom got up and was out of the bathroom, he approached, "mom don't forget to get an update on Liz as soon as you get to the main house."
Lucy smiled at her worried son and touched his cheeks, "everything will be ok my dear sweet and caring child, I

spent most of my night praying and I know my God answers prayers. I will get an update as soon as the Mrs awakes and I will let you know, Ok?"

He nodded his approval. While he waited, he decided to take out the goats and refill the water barrels that were running low. He also helped his father with some yard chores to keep his mind occupied.

At eight when his mom had prepared and served breakfast at the main house, she came back with the good news. Elizabeth's injuries were not life threatening. They were running more test, but she would be fine.

"Mom, can I ride my bike down to the hospital to see her?"

"Not today sweetie. If she is there for an extended time we can call a taxi and go for a visit."

"Ok. I am going to my room to prepare a get-well card for her. I'll give it to her mom when she's ready to leave for the hospital"

"While you're at it, whisper a prayer on her behalf, God will work it out."

Tafari walked off to his room wishing she was coming home today, however grateful that she only had some tests to do. He prayed that the test results were good so she could come home. Things would not be the same without her presence on the farm. She treated everyone like family. Her melodious voice lingered long after she had said, good morning, like a song with an endless tune.

About midday, a taxi arrived to take the Blackwoods to the hospital. Tafari boldly walked up to Mrs. Blackwood and handed her the get-well card he had made for Liz. "Good

afternoon madam. Could you please give this to Liz for me and tell her I said, get well soon."
She held on tightly to the note as if it gave her hope and answered, "I will son."
Son, Did she just say son? Tafari thought as he stared at the vehicle going down the driveway. He must be hallucinating. He could never have heard right, "Son," he repeated to himself. If he had heard right, that could mean she was now seeing him as a potential boyfriend for her daughter. He smiled at the thought.
"Are you going to stand around daydreaming or, are you going to get some work done around here?"
"I vote to daydream." He looked at his mom laughing and Lucy couldn't help but join in.
"Mom, I just handed Mrs. Blackwood a card for Liz and she called me 'son'. Do you think....?"
Her expression quickly changed. "No son, I don't think." She spoke in the same tone she would use whenever he was in trouble, so he knew she was serious. "Tafari, my son don't set yourself up for failure. The day will never come when they accept us as one of them or accept you as an eligible partner for their daughter."
Tafari hung his head and walked away, his heart filled with sadness at his mother's words. She always had such faith in him, so these words coming from her were like a thorn to his soul. How dare she give up on him now? How could she believe that he could never be good enough for Elizabeth? He knew he was, now he had to find a way to prove it to everyone.

Chapter Six

"Doctor, what's the latest on my daughter, Elizabeth Blackwood?"
The doctor turned around to find the direction of the question. "I beg your pardon, but who are you folks?"
"I am Loviet Blackwood and this is my husband Stan Blackwood. We are her parents Doc."
"Forgive me, but my reason for asking is that there was another gentleman asking about her earlier.
To quote he said to the nurse, "I would like to know the status of my daughter Elizabeth. We were in an accident together."
"Oh, it must have been John. He is a dear family friend and our driver all through the years. He was driving last night when they had the accident."

She knew John may have gone to the nurse claiming to be Elizabeth's father as he cared for her dearly and knew sensitive information would not be divulged to anyone except the parents.
His daughters were also in the car, but were treated and sent home, so she could see where he would be worried about Lizzie.
She did not mind that he claimed to be her dad as she would have done the same thing given the situation.
"That's all good and well doc, we'll talk to John about it but for now, could you please update us with the latest on our baby."

"The test results show that the bump on her forehead has caused blood clotting in that area but she will heal very well after a few weeks."
His expression changed to one of worry. "What worries me the most is the psychological stress she may face after this. Even with sleeping aids she did not sleep well last night. The nurses on night duty reported this morning that she had awoken several times screaming as if reliving the accident. I'll watch her to determine if she should be given antidepressants"
She had even wet the bed but he withheld that piece of information as he didn't wish to cause her parents any more worry than they already had. "I know this will be fresh in her memory for a while so family support is very important. We will do a few more tests between today and tomorrow to ensure there are no underlying injuries that did not come up in the x-rays."
He pointed her parents to the direction of her room, "you can go in and say hello, but try not to have her talking for too long as she will be drowsy from the sedatives I prescribed this morning. I will have more details for you before the day ends."

John was sitting in a chair in the room, lost in thought. He sprung unto his feet at their appearance. Mr. Blackwood tapped him on his shoulder with a friendly, "What's up old friend? I've got to touch you gentle as I know old boys like us don't heal quickly."

John laughed for the first time since the ordeal. "Hope I didn't cause any trouble out there, as no one would give me any details on Lizzie's well-being so I claimed to be her dad. I was worried sick about her."

"We understand, after all, you are her uncle. You know I see you as a brother. Right?"

"Mom, Dad, is that you?"
"Yes baby, it is." Pulling closer to Lizzie's bed and holding on to her hands, her mom gently whispered, "are you ok my sweet? I heard you didn't sleep well last night."
"I just need to rest, I'll be fine. Does Tafari know I was in an accident?"
"Yes he does." Loviet pulled the note from her purse. "He asked me to give this to you."
For the first time since the accident Liz cracked a drowsy smile. "Open it for me please."

Inside it read,

I wish I could send you a chocolate or a rose
My heart is willing, but my pocket is broke
So for now, please accept this note
Get well soon my sweet sugar cone

Love Tafari

Liz held the note to her face and if she could smell him, and whispered, "Thank you"
Her mom looked on without a word.

She soon fell asleep, still holding the piece of paper as if it brought her peace. Stan stepped out shortly after to get them lunch.

Loviet was standing there staring down at her daughter considering how blessed she was that her baby's injuries were not severe when the voice came up behind her. "Is he gone?"

She turned around to see John standing there. Her piece of mind quickly changed to annoyance, "If by 'he' you are referring to my husband then yes, he has stepped out to get us lunch."

"We need to talk Lov."

"What could be so important that it must be discussed at the side of my daughter's sick bed John? And by the way, how dare you claim to be Elizabeth's father to get information on her? Were you even considering my husband's feeling with your actions?"

"Are you saying I should not be concerned about my daughter's health Loviet? She could have died not knowing who her real father is."

Loviet pulled the curtains to her daughter's bed, "Control yourself John, and you need to speak softly. What if Stan walks in and hears you? Or God forbid my baby girl should awake. Is this the best time you could think of to have this conversation?"

"She is way under from the sedatives so she won't get up, but I need to know your intentions. How long do you plan on keeping this a secret? It is eating away at my soul. I want to tell my wife and the girls so badly, and now that we could have lost her, I guess.."

"I fully intend to take this secret to my grave John. What do you mean how long I plan to keep it?" Loviet cut in, not giving him a chance to complete his statement. "Why would I risk losing my husband? Why would you risk losing your wife and kids over this?"
"But she is my daughter. What if she needed a blood transfusion?" Who would give her blood? Do you think I would sit around and watch my daughter die to save your reputation? Stan may be my lifelong friend and the last thing I would want to do is hurt him, but I can't hold this any longer, I need to let her know that I am her real father."

Stan was her real father, the only father that mattered. She was thankful to John for giving her the one thing her husband couldn't, but she would not allow him to take away everything she had.
He was blessed with two beautiful girls and a lovely wife, she couldn't comprehend why he would want to tear her family apart. Stan loves his daughter and would give his life for her, that's what truly mattered, not the blood type that ran through her veins.
"And how do you suggest I tell the man I have loved since I was only a teenager, that after years of trying to be pregnant, I had given up on the thought that we would ever be parents, that in a moment of weakness, I confided in his best friend who comforted me and got me pregnant?" Loviet looked at him with tear-filled eyes and trembling lips. "Our relationship could never withstand the hurt, he would leave me for sure."
John stretched out his hand and nestled them on her shoulders, looking her directly in her eyes, before saying in

a low tone "If he leaves, we would finally be free to be together, we could have a son together and raise our girls as a happy family." He took a deep breath and shook his head. "The girls and I are blessed to have Marlene in our lives but truth be told, I have fallen out of love with my wife a long time ago. The night I spent with you fifteen years ago was the best night of my life," he paused to see her reaction.

"I still feel your warmth as you yielded to my touch. The scratch marks you left behind are buried beneath my skin. I will never forget your taste, your smell, how you screamed as you orgasmed. You told me you had never cum like that with him before."

He used one hand to lift her cheek. "Why would you punish yourself being in a relationship that doesn't allow you to be all the woman you were meant to be?"

"Are you crazy?" Loviet shot at him, her tone as steel. "Why would I want to do that? Why would I leave my mansion to come and be with you in that hut you call a home? Your damn neighbours can hear everything through the cracks in the boards" Her look filled with disdain as she continued her assault. "My daughter goes off to medical school within a few years, who will finance her? Can you even afford the plane ticket to get her from Jamaica to study in Pennsylvania?"

She paused as if giving him a chance to answer before pouncing on. "If I am with you I will have to start working again." The scorn was apparent in her tone and the way she looked at him. "We both know the reason Marlene had to leave for work in the states is that you could not maintain the children on what you earn. Furthermore, you would lose the pay check that you now get from my husband for being our family driver. Do I look as if I want to live as a pauper?"

With that she pointed towards the door, "please, leave my daughter's hospital room and don't visit again until she gets home and your visits can be properly monitored."

She decided then that she would also need to get a new driver to take Elizabeth to and from school as she didn't trust John not to tell her the truth. She had to protect her family from this information as its release would cause irreparable damage to their happy home.

She knew Liz would want to know the reason she changed drivers, but she would find a way to explain him away. She had no other choice.

"May the hands of God rain down on you Loviet!" These were John's final words before storming out of the hospital room. The pain she saw in his eyes before he left made her regret some of the things she had said, but this secret had to remain, as its release would have crippling effects, not just on their home but, Stan's reputation as a respected farmer would be ruined.

 In the restroom, Loviet tried to wash her tears away so her husband would not see that she was crying. She asked God to forgive her for her error. How could she explain this to her husband? How could she ever explain this to her baby? They would both hate her and no doubt she would lose them for good. This secret had to be taken to her grave. There was no other way.

"Dad, I think I may have wet the bed". Elizabeth held on to her dad's hands as he walked into the hospital room and placed the lunches on the table next to her bed.

"I am so sorry baby. I understand. It's because you are sick, it's not your fault. Couldn't you have called out to your mom to take you to the restroom? Wasn't she here with you when I stepped out to get lunch?"

"She was, but I didn't want to interrupt her conversation with Uncle John." Elizabeth sucked in a sharp breath to stop herself from crying.

"What could have been so important that you were afraid to interrupt?" He felt his daughter's grip tighten on his hand and he realized then she was trembling.

"Are you coming down with a fever?" He placed the back of his hand to her neck.

"No dad, I am not," her voice now cracking with her tears. "That's not it. You need to talk to mom"

"Speak to me about what?" Just then Loviet walked into the hospital room. Her daughters face held a look she had never seen before. "Are you trembling baby, do you have a fever?" Stretching her arm out to place it on her daughter's neck.

"Don't touch me!"

"Elizabeth," her dad reprimanded. "How could you talk to your mom like that? Apologize immediately, being sick is no excuse for disrespecting the woman who gave you life."

"I'm sorry dad, but when you hear what she has done you will feel the same way I do, I hate her."

"I think it may be the medication Stan. It must be affecting her mentally. Let me get the doctor." She stepped towards the door.

"You liar, you know exactly what I am talking about and if you don't tell him, I will."

Loviet was stopped dead in her tracks. Oh my God, she heard, "what will I do now?" She couldn't find the answer to her question, so she guessed she had no other choice but to turn around and face the music, whatever the consequences. Tears ran down her cheeks. She turned around to look at her daughter, "I am so sorry baby, you know I would never intentionally hurt you nor your dad. I love the two of you more than life itself."

"Can someone fill me in on what's happening here? What have you done? What could have caused our baby to have such a meltdown? I have never heard her talk to anyone like that, not even the men who work the farm."

"Could we please talk about this when she comes home from the hospital? This needs to be done in private."

"No, we can do it now, that 'home' that you are referring to, belongs to me and my dad, not a deceiver like yourself."

"Elizabeth Blackwood! Not another word from you. I don't care what your mom has done, you have no excuse to speak to her like that. Loviet, get the nurse, the medication has to be getting to her head. They need to do something, this isn't my baby."

The nurse walked in shortly after, pulling a tray behind her. "Please step outside so I can check if she's running a fever. Some of these medications can have serious side effects. They have been known to cause hallucination and irate behaviour. I will flush her and give her something to sleep." The nurse looked at them standing in the doorway. "This means she will have to stay here a few more days for observation, but don't worry, she will be fine. Continue to pray for a speedy recovery."

"Thank you, nurse. Can her mother stay and tidy her up? She had wet the bed earlier."
"No! I don't want her to touch me with her lying, conniving hands. You stay and tidy me up daddy"
"That's ok Mr. Blackwood. We have someone to do that. Just step outside so we can get to work."
"Tell him, tell him, he deserves to know, tell him you witch." Elizabeth cried as her parents walked out.
"Oh my God." Stan placed his hands over his mouth. "What could have happened to rile up my baby in that fashion? Let's go down to the chapel and breathe a prayer for her. It's as if she has been possessed by demons. Oh God help us."
They walked quietly to the chapel and after praying, Stan took his wife by the hands. "I have never seen that look in my daughter's eyes or hear her speak like that to anyone before, and even though I was told the medication can affect her, I still have to ask, what were you and John discussing earlier that could have triggered this behaviour?"
Loviet thought about it for a minute before answering. If she played this card right, she may not need to tell Stan after all, and her marriage would be safe. She would also need to convince Elizabeth that it was only the medication that was playing tricks on her, and that what she thought she heard was not the case.
"You heard the nurse Stan, she is being affected by the medication and may be hearing things. John and I spoke about the accident and I mentioned I was going to get a new

driver because I don't believe he took the proper precautions which led to the accident."

"That's preposterous Lov, and you know it. John has been our driver since we have been together. You know I would never get around a steering wheel, I trust the man with my life. He would never do anything to harm Elizabeth, furthermore, his kids were in the car."

"Well I don't trust him anymore and I would prefer to get another driver. I don't want to worry about her when she leaves for school. I'll ask my brother to come and stay at the great house, he can be our new driver."

"So that's it? One accident is all it takes to write off a long-time friend and driver?" He looked at her with raised eyebrows. "Loviet, you broke down in the hospital room telling our daughter you didn't mean to hurt us, and now you stand here before God lying to me? I know there is something else and if I can't get it from you, I'll ask John." He moved towards the exit of the chapel. "As a matter of fact, I think he's still here."

Loviet grabbed hold of her husband's hands. Somehow, she thought, it would be better if he heard it from her, maybe, just maybe, she could get him to forgive her for this error.

She sighed deeply and hung her head before beginning, "My dear husband, please know that I never meant to hurt you. I have loved you since I was a young girl. You were my first, my only true love."

She fetched a breath before continuing. "We had been trying for years to have a child and even with multiple visits to a fertility specialist, I had not become pregnant." She now lifted her head to face him. "I became depressed, I blamed myself for not being able to give you the one thing that would complete our family. You had given me everything, and I was unable to give you the one thing that would complete you, someone to call you dad."

"Oh honey"

"No, let me finish. I started taking anti-depressants, because I struggled with suicidal thoughts. Dr. Stephens was sworn to secrecy and I hid the medication from you."
She paused, searching for strength to continue. "One night when I was at the lowest and John was taking me home from school, I started talking to him about what I was going through. To add to my sorrow, his wife had just shared the news that they were expecting, and whilst I knew I should have been celebrating with her, I had a mental breakdown." Even now she could feel lingering guilt. "That night she was in Kingston with her family and you were overseas so we drove to his place to talk." She tightened the hold on his hands for support. "After having a few glasses of brandy, I started to relax. He even managed to make me laugh. He came on to me, but I did nothing to stop him. I needed to be held that night. I am so sorry."
Her tears flowed loosely. "When I found out that I was pregnant, I convinced myself it was yours. Deep in the back of my head, I knew it couldn't be but I just lived believing that everything would be ok, and that this wouldn't come to light. You were so happy when you found out; you said it was the best day of your life. I decided then that this error would go with me to my grave."
She paused for a while searching her husband's face for some sign of emotion. He didn't seem angry, but she could

not tell what he was thinking. "Say something Stan, shout at me. Tell me you hate me, anything, but not this, not silence."

He sat quietly for another few minutes before taking his wife by the hands and leading her to the seats nearby. He thought about what to say and how to say it before he began, "I have a confession to make to you too."

Oh no, this could not be good. What confession was Stan going to make? Was he going to confess that he had another family overseas and that when he was there, he was with them? She always had her suspicions because sometimes he would leave for months and she wasn't able to accompany him as she didn't wish to be away from Elizabeth for so long. She imagined her world falling apart if that was his revelation. She understood exactly how he must feel, finding out that his daughter he had spent the last fourteen years loving and taking care of, was not his, 'biologically', she reminded herself. Now she would lose them both. How could she ever go on without them?

She opened her mouth to break the silence but he held a finger up to his lips, so she remained quiet, waiting, trying desperately to decipher his emotions.

After a few more torturing minutes, he finally broke the silence, "The truth is Loviet, I always knew she wasn't mine."

She looked at him wide-eyed, too shocked to speak.

"You see, I had a terrible car accident when I was a child. That's the reason I would never drive. My dad had just bought a 1940 Bentley Mark V and decided to take me and my mother out to see a show on December night, around the time they celebrated Christmas. That night he had a

little too much to drink and on our way back to the plantation, there was a horrific accident."
The memory was still painful. He had never shared the full details of the accident with his wife as he preferred to bury the memory. "Thankfully, no one died, however, my injuries were so severe doctors said I wouldn't walk again."
Stan continued to explain that he had spent most of his childhood years in a wheelchair and that miraculously, at age ten, he started making small steps until eventually he started walking again. When he was sixteen he started feeling intense groin pains and was taken to the doctor, and after multiple test, the doctors concluded he was at risk of developing cancer if he didn't remove one of his testicles. He was flown abroad to have the surgery which was successful but, he was told then that his chances of having any children were minute.
"When we got married and I saw how badly you wanted a baby, I started visiting a specialist overseas, that's the reason I was gone for months sometimes."
He explained the various test and minor procedures that the fertility doctor conducted to see if his sperm would survive long enough to allow for fertility. They always died after a short period, proving without a doubt, he could not get a woman pregnant.

"When you told me you were pregnant, I contacted my doctor with the exciting news and he quickly wrote back to tell me there was no way I could have possibly impregnated you." His expression changed to one of sadness. "I held on to faith, hoping and praying that he was wrong and that this was another miracle." He looked away from his wife's face before continuing, "When she was born I contemplated doing a DNA test but decided I would only be hurting myself if she turned out not to be mine." He sighed heavily, "As she grew, and I saw how much she had in common with John's eldest daughter, the way they spoke alike, they looked alike; they were practically twins. That's when I put the pieces together. I was very upset with you for choosing someone so close to home, but I could not ignore how happy she made you. Seeing the light return to your eyes, I had no choice but to forgive you and to forgive John."

He guessed he always knew the day would come when the truth would come to light and he was prepared. "Though it really hurts to know that you found comfort in my best friend and that he gave you something I couldn't, I have forgiven you a long time ago. I would never wish for you or Elizabeth to be out of my life. You two ladies complete me. I love you Loviet."

This was the best thing she had heard in all her life. Tears flowed from both their faces as she took her husband's hands and held it to her face. "You and Elizabeth are the best parts of my life too and I would die if I lost you. How will she ever forgive me for this Stan?"

"She loves you and one day she will understand. Just take it slowly. She will eventually come around, plus I will talk to her."

"You heard her in there, she hates me. She called me deceptive." New tears filled her eyes. "I wouldn't have forgiven my mother if I found out she had lied about my father. I am truly saddened about this Stan. She will never forgive me for this." She took a deep breath before shifting to another important question, "What are we going to do about John? He was demanding that I tell Elizabeth that he is her biological father."

"John is my best friend and will continue to be if that's what he wants, but I will not allow him to come between me and my family. I will set him straight."

"They sat quietly for a few minutes just holding each other, forehead to forehead, she whispered, "I love you" and sealed it with a kiss. "Now let's go talk to Elizabeth"

"I believe I need to talk to her alone. Let's have the driver take you home. When you get there, have Lucy cook you a nice meal and get some rest. I'll be there in a few hours." He walked her to the exit and ensured she was off safely before returning to his daughter's hospital room.

"Elizabeth honey, how are you feeling now? The nurse told me you were awake and asking for me. Are you up for a talk or would you prefer we talk tomorrow after you are rested?" The last thing he wanted was to add unnecessary stress to her.

 "Dad, I don't want to lose you." As soon as the words were out, tears followed. "Will I have to leave and live with Uncle John? I hate mom for doing this to us. I don't want to leave," she sobbed.

"My baby girl, my sweet baby girl. I am the only dad you have and will ever have. You are not going anywhere, and neither is your mom. She made a big mistake, but that's what it is, only a mistake, and from that mistake something wonderful was created. Something I had waited for all my adult life. You are the best gift I have ever received in my entire life." He looked her directly in her eyes, ensuring he had her full attention. "I can tell you one thing for sure, your mother loves you with all her heart and all her soul and if she was to lose you, she would die. I know it's a lot to take in and that you feel deceived by your mom, but I pray you find it in your heart to forgive her because I have. It may take a while, but promise me, you will try."

"So you are not upset with her?"

"I am upset about the way you found out because they should have been more careful not to have that conversation around you." He touched her face before continuing. "To tell you the truth Elizabeth, I always knew you were not my biological child."

He held her hand to offer additional comfort. "It really didn't matter to me who fathered you, as I was unable to give your mom the one thing she wanted more than anything in this world, a child. What mattered was that you brought joy to our lives. You healed your mother from years of depression and made me into something I had always wanted to be.

"What's that?"

"A very proud dad" Elizabeth smiled at this. I love you Elizabeth and I love your mom very much. The two of you are the best parts are my life."

She lifted his hand to her cheek. "I am very happy to hear you say that dad, and I will try to forgive mom. I don't promise it will be tomorrow, but I promise to try."

That's the best he could ask of her as he understood how hard it could be to forgive someone who has hurt you immensely.

This lie had the power of tearing their family apart, had he found out after almost fifteen years later. He was glad he had found out when he did as he may not have been so forgiving otherwise. "What will you do about Uncle John?

His daughter's question broke through his thoughts. "He was demanding that mom allow him to be a part of my life. He even asked that we come and live with him."
"I'll have a talk with my dear old friend John. You try not to worry about it, you and your mom are going nowhere. I know you are very close with his children and I wouldn't dare keep you away from them, however I am agreeing with your mom that maybe he should not be taking you to school at this time. Your mom will ask your uncle to come and be our driver for a while."
"Ok dad, I am going to get some rest now. You talk a lot, do you know that?" They both laughed so hard, a nurse peeked in with finger on her lips as a signal that they needed to be quiet. He gave his daughter a kiss on the cheek and said good night.

"How is my baby?" Loviet was still awake when her husband got home.
"She is fine. We had a long talk. She was worried that you would be leaving to live with John, but I assured her that will never happen and she's now getting some rest. How are you doing my love? Have you eaten?"
"I tried, but I couldn't get the food to pass this lump in my throat, so I gave up."
"Let me make you some of your favourite oatmeal porridge, join me in the kitchen. I'll tell you about the talk I had with John on the drive home."
"He drove you home? Wasn't his car totalled?"
"Yes," he is driving his brothers Peugeot. I saw him outside the hospital when I was leaving. He looked so confused."

"Ok, I'll join you."

She watched as her husband took out all the ingredients needed to make the porridge. She kissed her lucky charm her grandmother gave to her as a child. It must be working for God to have given her such a blessing in the form of her husband. He was by far the best gift she has ever gotten, next to her daughter of course. "Thank you Jesus," Loviet whispered.

"Amen."

They laughed together as she did not know her husband was hearing the quiet conversation she was having with the most high. The laughter was well-needed healing for her soul.

The porridge was ready in a few minutes and her husband dished two bowls and sat down across from her. "So, I told John that we will be pulling the driving services from him for a while to give him a chance to gather his emotions."

Stan understood his friends' emotional state, after all, he had not seen his wife in over a year. He begged his friend to try harder to save his marriage. He knew loneliness was no bliss, especially for a man who was used to having the warmth of a woman in his bed. "John understands that I love my family and that I will never let anything or anyone come between us. I offered to pay for his ticket to spend two weeks with his wife in the states." His wife nodded her agreement. "The girls can stay with us as we have the guest room they can occupy. He leaves in a week. Elizabeth should be home by then and remember, her fifteenth birthday is coming up, so we can throw a party. That should help her to heal just fine." His expression suddenly became stern, "John was also warned that if he makes a pass at my wife again, it will not go down so easily."

Smiling from cheek to cheek, she held out her hands. Let's go upstairs. I have something to show you."

"Yes boss" They laughed as he took his wife's hands.

Chapter Seven

The next few days were uneventful. They made their routine visits to the hospital to see Elizabeth. She spoke very little to her mom. She mainly asked about the workmen, Tafari, and Aunt Lucy. On the day she was due to come out, Loviet invited Tafari to come along as she knew this would make Elizabeth very happy and would be a score for her on the forgiveness card.

He got up early, put himself together nicely, picked some fresh flowers and was waiting in the driveway when the Blackwoods stepped out. He was looking quite dapper. Loviet could see why her daughter would be in love with him. He took real pride in his appearance.

She quickly shunned the thought of her daughter being in love with the son of the help. That could never be, not as long as she had anything to say about it, but for now, she was willing to accept that seeing him would put some light back into her daughter's eyes.

He looked pretty tense so she thought she would lighten the air. "Oh Tafari, You look so sharp. Did you put yourself together or was it your mom?"

He smiled. "No mam, this was all me," his face lit up with pride.

"Very nice. Ok, hop in. She pointed to the car"

The hospital was a few miles from home. Except for the bad roads, the view was stunning. They had been having days of rain and as a result, everything looked so green and alive. The sugar fields whistled sweet harmonies as they drove by. He was amused to see a mongoose shooting across the road. He whispered, "God bless my eyes" as this was the tradition, whenever you saw one.

He thought about what he would say to Elizabeth when he saw her.

"I can't tell you how much I have missed you
Your smile, your charm, the sweet melody in your voice as you hum your favourite tune
The way you say ' Good morning always makes my day
My days haven't been the same since you've been away
I guess this is what I'm trying to say, don't ever leave because without you my life would be incomplete."

He wasn't one to toot his own horn but, he must admit, he could charm a turtle out of his shell, self-admiration radiated as he smiled to himself.

"We are here", Loviet announced. "Tafari, you stay out here, we'll go and sign her out and pack her stuff. She will be so happy to see you. I can't wait to see her smile again."

"Yes, mam." He watched as they walked away and he could finally let out the breath he held the entire trip. It was a tense ride being in the same space as Mr. and Mrs. Blackwood.

"Let's go sit under that tree." He was so deep in thought, he didn't realize the driver had come up behind him. Tafari had never seen him before, he imagined he must be a friend of the Blackwoods. He seemed to be a gentleman so Tafari had no reservations for sitting with him.

They walked to the shade and before Tafari could find a place to sit, the gentleman asked, "So what's the deal, are you the boyfriend of this young lady they are picking up today?"

Tafari realized then that he could not be a friend of the Blackwoods as he didn't even know Elizabeth's name. He must be a hired driver as Tafari was told John's car was totalled in the accident. "Boyfriend," he repeated with a smile. "I wish, I am merely the son of the helper. These people will never accept me as anything but."
"Is that how you see yourself son? Will you be merely the son of the help or will you be what God ordained you to be? Will you fulfil your own destiny? Will you become someone this young woman can be proud to call a husband or, are you content with the classification given to you by her parents?"
Tafari thought about the profound words of wisdom coming from this stranger. He wasn't sure if he had been chartered for the day or if he was here to take John's place until he could purchase a new car, but the questions he asked were profound. It was just what Tafari needed to hear at this point in time.

His mom always told him, the lord can send an angel to guide you through the darkest hours. He looked up at the gentleman looking intently back at him and answered, "I will sir, I promise, I will."
The hospital door pushed open just then and an orderly came out with his love in a wheelchair. He walked up to the end of the steps, flowers outstretched. "Flowers for my flower"

She looked up and realized Tafari was standing there, and with one leaping motion she threw her arms around his neck, planting a sweet kiss on this cheek. "You are here, you are really here. Have you any idea how badly I have missed you?"

He shifted a little from her grasp before answering, "well if I am to judge from the way you are choking me, I would say, a lot." They laughed as Lizzie loosened her grip on his neck just a little. "And would you believe I missed you more? Nothing has been the same without you there."

Her parents stood by watching. Loviet didn't wish to say or do anything to spoil this perfect moment as she saw the smile return to her daughter's eyes for the first time in weeks. After a few more minutes however, she announced "Ok guys, let's take her home."

"Mom, can we stop for ice cream on the way?" I am longing for a double cone vanilla with sprinkles. I'm sure Tafari would love one too."

"Sure, we can stop at Charlie's ice cream place. I'm sure we could all do with some ice cream." They all nodded their approval.

Everyone, including the driver, got double cones. Tafari and Elizabeth walked to a bench that gave well-needed shade from the overhead sun. They chatted for what seemed like forever. She spoke of her experience with the doctors, nurses, and orderlies. She explained how everyone took really good care of her. An orderly even washed and combed her hair in preparation for her release this morning. "You look as if you are coming back from a two weeks' vacation."

She smiled, leaning her head on his shoulder. "You really know how to make a girl blush, don't you? I wonder if that's how you speak to all girls."

"I am only speaking the truth. There's no other girl that makes me feel the way you do Liz, I really think I may love you."

With that she just held on to his hand, gently squeezing, that motion speaking the thoughts of her heart.

"Do you remember when we were like that?" Stan caught his wife off guard with his question.

Loviet had been deep in thought, thinking that her daughter could very well be in love with this young man. After all, she fell in love when she was pretty young.

Her thoughts had explored, what he would grow up to be. He was a bright boy, but who would send him to university? Could he be anything but a farm hand like his dad? Playing reggae music, dancing and singing along with his un-kept hair falling over his shoulders and smoking marijuana as his pass-time? The odds were against him. What well-thinking mother could want that for her child? God forbid.

"Yes, I do, but I will never support a relationship between my daughter and that boy. What kind of life will he be able to give her? She is going to be a doctor and what will he be, a natty head Rasta who burns weed? Over my dead body."

"Remember she is our only child so when we die, the plantation is rightfully hers. She will need a strong man with a knowledge of farming to be by her side."

"Are you planning to die soon, because I'm not? So what do you suggest, that she sit around hoping we die so that she and her man will inherit our estate? I'm sorry, but I can't agree to that," she lashed.

"I see this is a touchy topic so we'll stop here. Get the kids so we can go home."
The journey home was a tense one. When they reached the great house Lucy rushed out to meet them. She had not seen Elizabeth since she had been in the hospital, sadly she never got a chance to visit.

She gave Liz a big hug as she exited the car. "Girly, am so sorry I couldn't come to the hospital to see you, but you know I missed you right? I prayed for you every day. Did they take good care of you? Turn around so I can see if you've lost any weight." She continued without a break, "Come, I have made your all-time favourite, ackee and saltfish with white rice and fruit punch juice."
She followed excitingly behind her nanny, giving her experience in the hospital. She could not say what had taken place between her parents and Uncle John because they were around, but as soon as they went up, she planned to confide in Aunt Lucy.
They all had lunch, including Tafari and then went their separate ways. Loviet and Stan went upstairs to rest as they were exhausted. They encouraged Elizabeth to do the same as they knew she must also be pretty tired and longing to lay in her own bed.
Elizabeth opted to help Aunt Lucy clean up the kitchen as they had some catching up to do. Her parents knew she was very fond of her nanny so they let her be.

Aunt Lucy washed the plates while Elizabeth rinsed, dried and packed.

Elizabeth's question interrupted her humming, "Aunt Lucy, did you know that dad isn't my real father?"

She looked at Elizabeth startled, then whispered, "Girl shhh, don't say that. Did you bump your head so hard that you've come back here talking foolishness?"

"But Aunt Lucy, it's true. I found out while I was in the hospital that Uncle John is my biological father."

She looked at Liz, saddened that she had found out the way she had. "My sweet baby girl, I am very sorry that you had to be faced with such a burden especially when you should have been recuperating. You are so young and innocent and you deserve to be protected." She sighed before continuing. "In a sense, I always knew, but it was never my place to say. I do understand the damage that can be done with such a revelation, but seeing that your father has found a way to forgive your mom, I would beg you to find it in your heart to do the same."

Liz looked and listened attentively. She held such high regards for the woman who has taken care of her since birth. She valued every word of wisdom coming from her nanny.

Lucy dried her hands on her apron and faced Liz. "Sweetheart, you are truly loved by both your parents. Your dad certainly does not care what blood type runs through your veins. He will always love you. I would beg you my dear to let this die here. The disgrace that would come to the estate if this ever gets out would be unbearable. Ok Lizzy?"

Coming from Aunt Lucy it made a lot more sense than it had coming from her parents. She thought about it for a moment, then with a deep sigh, she agreed.

Elizabeth spent the rest of the week in high anticipation of the girls' arrival. Uncle John brought them over the day before he was scheduled to leave for the states.
The two weeks they spent together was a ball. They played dress up like Barbie every night. They sang and performed, pretending to have a great big audience. Elizabeth allowed them to wear her clothes, her shoes and eat her snacks. She even taught them how to dance so they would be able to perform at her birthday celebration which took the form of a mini concert. All the workers and their children were invited to see them perform, including Tafari. Elizabeth had a blast that night. She couldn't remember ever having so much fun.
It felt really good having company that was the same age group around. She knew they were blood sisters, but she wasn't sure Uncle John had said anything, so she didn't. It made her feel so much closer to them as they were no longer just her driver's kids, but her sisters.
They had grown pretty close the two weeks they spent together. She even cried when it came time for them to leave. She begged Uncle John to ensure the girls came to visit more often. Her parents too were in full agreement as they too enjoyed having the girls around.
The good news was that Aunt Marlene had returned with Uncle John and she wasn't going back. She said she had realized the effect her absence had on her family and she didn't want them to fall apart. She was going to open a hair

salon in town and spend time rekindling the flames that seemed to have burned low in her marriage.

She also brought a lot of clothes and shoes for the girls, including Elizabeth. They were ecstatic that they would be able to dress like triplets whenever they went out.

Marlene told Loviet in private that her husband had confessed what had taken place between them fifteen years ago, and that she had forgiven him the moment he came clean. She explained she knew marriage was a lot of work and even more compromise and she was willing to do what it took to see her marriage run its full course.

She also mentioned that the girls would be told the truth about their relation to Elizabeth, but not today. They would decide on the right time. It was her hope the girls would get a chance to grow together.

Loviet agreed one hundred percent.

Chapter Eight

The next few years were spent focusing on achieving the best grades in her classes, as Liz and her parents had their eyes set on a Government scholarship that only accepted the best of the best from exam achievements.

Her new focus had robbed her of the opportunity to sneak across the fence to chat with Tafari, so she had to settle for an occasional hello and a charming smile whenever she saw him.

She wanted a lot more and was determined to get it too, but for now, she had to secure this scholarship. Once she was a medical doctor and her parents would no longer be able to control who she choose to spend her time with, then she could have Tafari all for herself.

Over the past two years, Elizabeth had struggled to forgive her mom and to rebuild their relationship. She merely spoke to her mom when there was a need, but the friendly mother daughter talks had been missing.

It wasn't until it was time for exam preparation that Liz really gravitated to her mom. In wee hours when the entire plantation was sleeping, her mom was up with her studying and ensuring and no stones were left un-turned. The fact that she was a retired teacher, she taught Liz every angle from which an examiner could approach a question.

She knew Elizabeth had the potential to get straight A's, and that a scholarship would be within reach, so they worked relentlessly towards this.

In the end, she was top girl in the island with twelve subjects, all A's. She made her parents very proud as was accepted by the University of her choice where she would be studying medicine. Things were really looking up for Elizabeth and she was fully embracing every aspect of it.

She could not believe the time had come for her to go off to University. She would be studying at one of the most prestigious Universities worldwide. She would be moving to Pennsylvania and boarding on campus too. Things were about to change for her really fast.

As per her parents' wishes, she would be pursuing a medicine degree, however upon research of the institution, she found that they had a top class dance faculty from which many renowned dancers had emerged. Though she could not tell this to her parents, she fully intended to minor in dance.

She couldn't stop thinking of Tafari and what would become of their friendship with them being so far apart. Over the past two years, it had driven Elizabeth crazy as she watched him grow into a stunning five feet eight inches, well build young gentleman and not being able to touch him nor share her thoughts with him. His hair had grown and now extended just above his firmly toned ass. His skin reminded her of rich chocolate, dark and mild.

He took great pride in his appearance, his favourite attire being cut jeans and marinas that barely hid his stacked chest with soft, curly hair peeking just above the neckline, showing off his irresistibly broad shoulders. His attire revealed way more than Liz would appreciate as she didn't want the girls in the community to get any ideas.

His feet were as clean as a baby's, his nails, though moderately tall were always clean, and best of all, he wasn't lazy, as young adults were known to be. He still helped his dad with yard chores and filled the water barrels for his mom.

Occasionally Liz would catch him shirtless coming in from his bathe at the nearby river and would gasp for breath, as she watched the water run gracefully down his back. He never bothered to dry with a wash cloth, as he preferred to sun dry. The water would take on the gleam of the evening sun, allowing him to illuminate like the angel he was. He was perfect.

Elizabeth never thought it was possible for her parents to become more protective, however, for the past two years they had become unbearably so.

This was because she had bloomed into a magnificent flower. Her breast rounded like apples ready for market, her skin as fresh water on rose, gentle and without blemish, small waist, broad hips, kitty grey eyes, straight nose and full lips.

She still wore her hair natural, but it could be finger combed as, it was really soft and tall. She mostly wore a bun as it complemented her round face perfectly. Elizabeth wasn't one to brag, but she had to admit, she was drop dead gorgeous.

Other young men in the community were now paying attention, even when she was out with her parents and that resulted in her being forbidden from standing at the fence to talk to friends as her mother would quickly call her away.

Tafari still spent most of his time in his tree-house practicing his drumming and guitar. He had a real guitar now. His mother had bought it on his sixteenth birthday. Liz stilled watched him occasionally through her bedroom window. She was yet to see the interior of the tree house, but not for long she promised herself, not for long. She was leaving in a few days and she knew she had to see the inside before she leaves.

She was excited about going away to school, but not about leaving Tafari. There would be more distance between them. Now they would not only be separated by a fence, there would be oceans between them. She couldn't leave without taking the chance to express her undying love for him.

In those instances when their paths would cross and she could not stick around to have a conversation, she could see the effect this had on him, she couldn't leave him with the impression that she no longer cared about him.

Tafari too had wondered many times what could have gone so wrong between himself and Elizabeth, why she was unable to spend two minutes to talk to him. It was heartbreaking to see her and not being able to talk to her, see her smile, nor hear her laugh.

This girl possessed him; like a skillful gig player, she had him wrapped around her fingers, with the power to let him down and reel him in.

He wondered if it was her parents that had managed to convince her to stay away from him. He bet they said he was no good. That nothing good could come of him. That he was just another Rasta boy who would roll up a spliff as

his pass-time, working on a farm, struggling to make his bread, walking in his father's footprints. If they ever knew his aim and his ambitions.
Music and dance was going to be his ticket to the world. He bet they would embrace him then. If they knew he saw himself on the cover of magazines, being featured on television programs, giving autographs and travelling the world.
When they realize his parents would no longer live and work on their farm, but would have their own. He bet they would accept him as being good enough for their daughter then.
He shook his head to free his mind of these thoughts, as he figured, they were not worth his energy. He would let his actions speak for themselves.

Tafari sat in his tree house staring at her window. Little did Liz know it was built with the perfect view of her bedroom.
He had watched her blossom from training bras to adult size. She was about '34c' now, he guessed. She had really firm buds. He had wondered so many times how it would feel to have them between his lips and his tongue.
He had seen her childish fat develop into curves. She now paid special attention to the panties she chose, what lip gloss matched her dress and how it all complemented her hairdo.
He remembered explicitly the first time he saw her in a thong, that night he had an erection so rigid, he thought he'd tear the sheets. When he closed his eyes, she was all he could see.

Her body was fit for a movie star, he thought, licking his lips. Whenever she wore red lip gloss, he always admired how well it highlighted her light caramel skin and kitty grey eyes.

At times when they had passed each other by, he would notice she smelled of beautifully scented perfume oils. The girl was absolutely breath-taking.

He knew she was still a virgin because her parents never allowed her to date, and everyday Uncle Charlie, her mother's brother and their new driver would take her to and from school. He wondered why Uncle John was no longer their chauffeur, but was never bold enough to ask.

She was the sweetest girl in town and she was his girl. No parents, no school and no ocean would keep them apart. This girl had a very special place in his heart.

He had waited patiently for the day he would make her a woman, his woman, and that moment was fast approaching. He made a promise to himself that before she left for college, he would lay claims on her.

His mother had told him she was accepted to a university in Pennsylvania and gave the date of her departure.

It was now two days before she would leave, so Tafari knew tonight was the night to make his move. He had it all planned out. He would wait until his parents were asleep. Watch until the lights went out in her parents' bedroom, give them an hour to fall deeply into sleep, then he would get her attention. For now, he would wait.

He took the opportunity to rid his face, underarms and pubic of excess hair. He spent a few extra minutes in the shower washing himself from head to toes. He used some of his dad's aftershave that made him smell manly and ensured his mouth was nice and fresh. He even used a little oil to ensure his lips were nice and soft. After that he spent some time listening to some music while working on his own lyrics.

Roses are red, violets are blue, sugar is sweet but not like you.

He laughed as he thought how corny he would sound if he used that cliché verse with her.
No, he had to have something genuine, something from the heart. He began again,

The first time I saw you Liz, I knew you were mine
I've watched you grow, I admire the way you glow and tonight, my love for you I want to show.

Yes, he shook his head, satisfied that he had found it. He felt nothing less than confident; tonight was the night.
It was now ten thirty. His parents had gone to bed at nine and the lights had gone off in her parent's room almost simultaneously. His thoughts at the time was that it must have been faith.
All lights were still off, so he took that to mean they were all sound asleep. This was the time to make his move. He took the ladder from his tree house, went to her window, leaned it against the wall and climbed up. He had wanted to do this so many times before, but he was always too scared. He knew Mr. Blackwood carried a gun and he didn't want to be mistaken for a burglar and to be shot. Tonight though,

he had to be brave, as this was his last chance to see her before she left.

"Liz," he whispered with a light tap on her window. To his surprise, he didn't have to call twice, as she quickly and silently slid the window open.
"Oh my God Tafari, Is that really you? Do you know how badly I've missed you?" She brushed a sweet little kiss across his lips. "Aren't you afraid of my dad?"
"Afraid?" He laughed nervously, still in a whisper, "I'm petrified, but I could not let you leave without seeing or touching you Liz."
"They say great minds think alike. I had this same intention to come to your window tonight," she smiled mischievously. "I couldn't leave without letting you know I lo.., love..," she struggled to get the words out.
"Let's go to my tree house, we need to be alone. I need to hold you before you leave."
Elizabeth wrapped herself in her dainty pink robe and followed Tafari down the ladder and up the tree house. As soon as they were settled he placed one hand on her hip and the other was used to lift her head.
"Do you know I've loved you even before I knew what it meant to love, Elizabeth?"
She was glad for the darkness so he could not see her cheeks burn. "I love you too Tafari," she whispered.

Tafari placed his warm, delicate lips on hers and started to caress them. As the kiss got deeper, she held on to him, kissing back as if her very breath depended on it.

His hands began to trace her neck then explored the rest of her body, landing gently on her breast. She wasn't wearing a bra so he could feel her tightly erected nipples. This made his body come alive with anticipation. She felt so damn good in his arms.

He could barely contain himself and his knees felt weak. He leaned against the board walls for support and pulled her closer so she could feel how badly he wanted her. He was rock hard.

He placed her hand on his manhood which was now bulging from his loose fitted pajama pants. He instructed her to touch him. She was a bit shy at first, but before long she had a steady rhythm.

He was about eight inches, she thought. He felt so rigid and it made her ache between her thighs. She wasn't sure she could take him, as he was large and she was still a virgin. She however trusted he would never hurt her.

She continued to caress his member in a circular motion until it became moist in her hands. He pulled away then as he couldn't take much more. One more minute of her sweet caress and he would have exploded in her hand. That was the last thing he wanted as tonight was her night and he would ensure she enjoyed every minute of it.

He continued to search her body, feminine curve after perfect feminine curve. He whispered, "you are so sexy." He continued to whisper how badly he wanted to make her into a woman. He loosened her bun and watched as her golden brown hair fell over her shoulders and was lit by the moon that peeked through the cracks in the ceiling. She was so damn perfect.

His hands had now found their way to her firm ass, he gripped it and lingered there for a while, caressing while kissing her dainty lips that now felt swollen from his assault, but he wasn't about to stop.

He could feel the effects from years of dancing as every inch of her body was so tight. It took all his efforts not to lay her down on the floor and take her right then and there.

He wanted her but he wasn't about to rush. She was a gem that deserved to be treasured.

He turned her around so her back was to him and turned his attention to her neck, kissing gently while his eager hands continued to explore. They made their way up her nighties and inside her panties. She was clean shaved and felt so warm.

He found her clit and started to caress it, she gripped his hands but didn't ask him to stop. He maintained a circular movement and within minutes she grabbed onto his thighs, as if holding on for support, then he felt why; her juices were warm and sweet on his fingers.

He inserted his index finger and basked in her sweetness. She was so tight. He wanted more, he wanted her to come again so her body would be prepared for him. He knew he was big and she was a virgin. She would need a lot of moisture to contend with what was about to come.

He knelt before her and started kissing her thighs, while maintaining a firm grip on her ass. She leaned against the board walls for support. He was careful not to go too far as he didn't want her to think he had this experience with any other girl.

He may not be sexually exposed but he had learned a lot from the Playboy magazine's his dad kept in his sock drawer, so he was ready for this moment.

His dad's brother who lived in the states sent the magazines by mail, and he hid them in his sock drawer as he thought his wife would not find them there. Tafari would borrow them in the evenings and took them to his tree-house to read and brought them back before dad got in from the farm. He was sure his mom knew they were there as you couldn't really hide anything from a woman.

He couldn't wait to show her the things he'd learnt. His caress intensified and he started whispering again, "I have dreamt of this moment a thousand times Liz, I always knew you would be my first and I would be yours."

His warm breath across her skin heightened her excitement and her nipples were now so hard they hurt. She looked down and took his chin in her hands. She had never been so sure about anything in her life, "I need you Tafari. I need to feel you inside me."

Those words were like gospel to his ears. He reached for a pack of condoms he had gotten in town earlier that evening and rolled one over his rigid member. It ached with need to be inside her lava filled center. He took her by the hand and led her to a sponge he had in one corner of the tree-house. He held her head and gentle laid her on her back.

Before he could join her there, she heard him utter under his breath, "Oh shit no!"

She couldn't find her words as she wondered why he would ruin this perfect moment with such an outburst. She wondered if he may have hurt himself and there she was acting selfish. Her feelings changed to that of concern. "What is it Tafari?"

"Liz, the lights just went on in your bedroom."

She felt hot and cold all at the same time. Her limbs felt dead, "oh my God, they are going to kill me."

"No, they won't. Just tell them you couldn't sleep, so you went for a walk."

"That will never work and you know it. One look and mom would know I'm lying. I've got to go before she starts calling. Goodbye Tafari."

"It's never goodbye Liz, it's see you later and remember, I will always love you."

She touched his face and without a word hurried down the ladder and towards the great house.

Chapter Nine

Elizabeth met her mother at the door.
She could see her mom was crying, "Elizabeth Blackwood, where were you?"
Elizabeth refused to answer. She didn't wish to lie to her mom.
"I am talking to you," Loviet said in a hardened tone.
Her father, who was in the shadows came to the door, "let's go inside, there's no need to wake the neighbours with this. You had better have a good explanation for your behaviour young lady," he reprimanded as they walked to the living room.
In the living room, her parents sat across from her, awaiting an explanation.
She sat quietly for a while, looking down at her hands, "I'm sorry mom, but I had to say goodbye to Tafari before I left for school."
"You did what?"
"I had to mom. He's the only true friend I've had since I was a little girl. He means a lot to me. You know I'm in love with him."
"Was a little girl?" her mother repeated with disgust. "Reality check, you are still a little girl. Did you have sex with him?" Loviet placed her hands across her eyes to stop from crying.
'No mom, I didn't." Elizabeth hang her head as she knew if she had gotten her will, this would no longer be true.
"Elizabeth Blackwood, look at me, I swear, if you had sex with that Rasta boy, you can kiss that scholarship and

university goodbye." She pointed a finger in Liz's direction. "I am taking you to the doctor in the morning and you better be a virgin. I don't know what we have done to deserve you as our child. Why do you want to disgrace your family Elizabeth?" Her mom started crying again.

Liz got up and walked towards for mom with the intention of reassuring her nothing happened but she looked up and snapped, "don't touch me, if you want to run around like a little whore, you are no longer my child, get out of my sight."

Her dad just sat there and said nothing. She couldn't tell whether it was out of fear for her mother, or if he was too ashamed of her to come to her defence. He was always in her corner, but not tonight, not when she really needed him.

She hated seeing her parents hurt like this. She walked away without another word.

Elizabeth couldn't help but feel heartbroken, she knew her parents loved her unconditionally, but her mom's words cut like a machete sharpened on both sides. She wished her mom could see Tafari for who he was, and the man he was going to be. His parents were poor, but he was destined for so much more.

He would be studying music and dance at an Art college in Kingston this September too. He had done very well in his studies and graduated with honours from his High school. A life on a farm was not going to be his reality.

She got to her room, took off her robe and dropped into bed, hoping sleep would relieve her from the turmoil in her head.

She was struggling with mixed feelings, happy they did not go all the way because she wanted to go to university, wanted to have a career, but on the other hand she wanted so badly to give him something to hold on to while she was away.

She wanted to express her love by giving him her virginity.

Even now, there was a longing, she could still feel the throbbing between her thighs. She needed a cold shower. Maybe that would soothe her longing.

Her eyes burnt as they filled up with tears. One day soon, she promised herself, one day soon. She just prayed Tafari would be willing to keep himself for her until that day.

After her shower, she thought about him a little while longer, until there was nothing but silence.

"Get up, get a shower, and get dressed." These were the words Liz got up to the next morning.

She opened her eyes to say good morning, but by then her mom had left the room.

She is really mad at me, Elizabeth thought. She got up, went to the bathroom, cleaned up and got ready. She made her way to the kitchen where Aunt Lucy was standing by the stove preparing breakfast.

"Good morning Aunt Lucy."

"Good morning Liz." Liz had never heard her nanny speak to her that stern before. The look on her face when she turned around confirmed that she was upset, "let me be clear Elizabeth, I do not condone what took place between you and my son last night. That could have meant a lot of trouble for Marcus and I."

Her voice trembled. "This job is what we depend on to provide for our family and with Tafari going off to college, we need this. You too acted very selfishly."

"I'm truly sorry Aunt Lucy, but if mom doesn't understand I expect you to, I love Tafari."
"Liz, I know all about love and I have no doubt that you do, however, this can never be, maybe in another life, in another place and time, but face it Lizzie, a Blackwood and a Messiah are from two different worlds. Stay in your lane Lizzie, I beg you."
Her heart broke all over again at those words coming from Aunt Lucy. She had expected some comfort from the one person who understood her more than her own parents did. She loved and trusted Aunt Lucy and always held high regards for words of solid wisdom.
Now, to hear her say that she should stay in her lane, as if she would never accept a relationship between Tafari and Liz, shattered her dreams like a ceramic vase hitting the floor.
She wanted to run to her room and cry her eyes out in her pillow however, she fought the urge to break. She was going to have Tafari and there was nothing their parents could do about it.
Elizabeth had lost her appetite. She stepped outside and waited for her mom under a shade tree in the front yard. She couldn't wait for this day and be over so she could get out of this place. She needed the break, but she was in no way giving up on her love.

Chapter Ten

Liz's was ready for her flight that would be departing Kingston any minute now. She hugged Uncle John, who had been given the opportunity to drive them to the airport. He didn't take along the girls nor Aunt Marlene as he had taken them to the plantation the night before to do their farewells.

She then hugged her dad and when she got to her mom, she held on to her hands and looked her in the eyes, "I love you mom and I pray you find it in your heart to forgive me".

Tears fell to her mom's cheeks as she pulled her daughter into her arms. "You are my miracle baby, I will always love you and yes, I forgive you. After all, you forgave me." They embraced a few more minutes then let go on the final boarding call.

Her mother's sister, Peggy would be meeting her at the Philadelphia International Airport and would drive her to the sorority house where she would be boarding for the next couple of years.

While in the air there was a nauseating feeling in the pit of her stomach. Excited about the prospects ahead but very sad about what she had left behind. She didn't know how she would get herself to stop thinking about Tafari every minute of every day.

Her aunt and cousins met her at the airport, took her for lunch, and then they drove her to her boarding house. She was quiet for the most part, as she could not get her mind off the events of the last few days.

They helped her with her luggage as she was staying on the third floor, and left with a promise that they would come back and show her around on the weekend.

She was glad her roommate had not yet arrived as she was not in the mood to talk. She took her time unpacking and reminiscing on her love back home. She decided to listen to one of the cassettes Tafari made and sent with his mom this morning before she left the great house.

Aunt Lucy had taken the opportunity to apologize for being so harsh the day before, but had also reminded her that she wasn't in support of a relationship between herself and Tafari. She however said she would not hinder them being friends.

They were lifelong friends and true friendship should be treasured. As soon as she pressed play on her little walk-man, her mood shifted to a more pleasant one as she heard his sweet voice;

This one is dedicated to the girl I love…

Girl, you drive me crazy with your smile
I am held captive for a while
Your eyes, your lips, your kiss, I will surely miss
The way your hair blows in the wind
How your hips flow like a hot, new rhythm
I am in a trance as I watch you dance.
Here I am wishing I'm the only man you'll give a chance
Girl I must confess, you had me at first glance.

She couldn't stop smiling as she listened to one dub poetry after another. She never knew he was this versatile. After a while, she could feel the exhaustion creeping in, she was happy the day was finally over.

It had been a long plane ride, especially since her heart was still in Jamaica. A million questions flooded her mind and added to her exhaustion. How could she leave him? How would she survive with them being oceans apart? Would he wait for her? Was there another girl waiting at the School of Arts that would swoop in and take her place in his heart?

Her parents had come to her room to have a chat with her the night before and had told her then, "Your whole life is ahead of you." They said she would forget all about Tafari as soon as she started making friends in the US, but Liz could never see that happening. Even now her heart broke into a thousand tiny pieces knowing she was so far away from him.
She laid down for a few minutes trying to clear her mind. She did not even hear the door open nor see her roommate come in.
"Hi, my name is Stacy, you must be Liz. When I heard I was going to share room with a Jamaican, I was super excited. I started practicing my Jamaican 'Ya man' 'Irie man' 'Wha gwan'. She went on without breaking, "Did you take any rum? Did you take any weed? We are going to have so much fun sharing this space and being very best friends. Oh my God!"

All this time Liz laid there silent, listening to Stacy blab. As for being best friends, she doubted that was possible. Her best friend was Tafari.

Hearing this girl go on and on with her preconceived notion that all Jamaicans drank rum and smoked marijuana made her even more home sick. She didn't attempt to correct her roommate, instead she remained quiet, pretending to be asleep until finally, there was nothing but blessed silence.

Liz woke up panting, frightened by the moisture she felt between her legs. She suddenly remembered the erotic dream she had. She was sitting on Tafari's lap with his sweet swollen member deep inside, as she screamed his name and scratched at his upper back. Warm rivers flowing between her legs.

Tafari whispering how warm she was and how he was about to explode, gripping her waist tightly to restrict the movement of her hips, as he could not hold out any longer. Just as they were about to reach climax, she awoke, feeling disappointed she wasn't able to share this moment with him. Even if it was only a dream.

Her nanny had told her once that whenever one goes to bed thinking of someone else, they were likely to dream about that person. Liz concluded this would be a regular thing as she could see herself thinking of Tafari every night.

She had never experienced a dream like this before. It felt so real. She felt dirty, but the throbbing between her legs felt really good. She couldn't wait for the day when her dream would become a reality.

She got up, looked at the time and realized it was just two in the morning. She decided to take a shower. Her knees were trembling so hard she could barely stand. This must be the feeling her friend Dianne had spoken about when she would share her sexual experiences with Liz.

While in the shower, she heard the door knock and before she could answer, it was pushed open and her roommate stepped in. "Hey Liz, I want to pee. I tried introducing myself last night but you fell asleep. I'm Stacy, you're roommate." She continued without awaiting a response from Liz. "I know it's late but I must say, I am super excited to be sharing a room with you and hope we can be new best friends. I want to hear all about you and your great island Jamaica. Anyways, good night, talk to you in the morning." She left without Liz getting a word in. Not that she wanted to anyhow. She always got along with everyone, but she could see where getting along with Stacy would be a challenge. It was really uncomfortable having someone in such an intimate space with her. That's one thing she never had to contend with at home, as she was an only child. She hated this arrangement. She would have to try pretty hard to conform to this change.

Liz finished her shower and went to the kitchenette for a snack. She loved St Mary's banana chips and so did Tafari. Liz sighed heavily, now every time she had chips she would think of him, every reggae song would be about him, every Rastafarian would look like him. Her eyes welled with tears. She decided to write him a letter telling him how badly she missed him.

Tafari my love,

My eyes burn with tears as I write this note
My heart fills with fear knowing you are not around
How will I bear knowing that we are oceans apart?
I may be here, but you have my heart.
I woke up trembling, calling your name
The place between my thighs as hot as flames
I lose all control to this burning desire.
Tafari, my love, please wait for me, for only you will be able
to quench this fire.

Yours faithfully,
Liz

She would mail it off to Jamaica in the morning, but until then, it will be sweet dreams about her love back home.

She knew she needed to rest as she would have her first class in the morning. She was warned she needed to brace for the racial divide. Her parents warned her about the stereotype given to Jamaicans in countries like the US. All Jamaicans drank rum and smoked weed.

They had however assured her that she would be ok. They reassured her, she was deeply loved by her family and friends back home. She would also be spending her weekends with Aunt Peggy and her cousins, so she could feel a family connection.

Chapter Eleven

It was now the end of the first school day and Elizabeth was relieved that it was over. If every class she went to had fifty students, only five were colored. A few other Caribbean students were in her classes but thus far, she was the only Jamaican. If she would be honest, the day ran pretty smoothly, except for a few upturned noses when she entered to the cafeteria that day.

The teachers were pretty pleasant, a few mean lunch-mates would not kill her. She would get used to it after a while and would learn to stay in her lane. She smiled at that phrase, as she recalled the morning Aunt Lucy had used it with her. It had been heart-breaking but she wouldn't have traded the experience of the night before for the world. She anxiously awaited the day they would go all the way.

The first few weeks ran off pretty well. A day had not passed that Elizabeth did not think about Tafari. She wrote a letter to him every night and mailed it in the mornings before school. She was surprised how well she had adjusted to her new environment. She even made a few friends, mostly from the other Caribbean countries, but much to her surprise, there were whites who invited her to sit with them at lunch.

They all wanted to hear about her culture, what she did for fun in Jamaica and how well she liked America. "I guess it's not as bad as everyone made it seem" was the answer she gave her Trinidadian friend Mary when she had asked her why she was being so friendly to all those white people.

Elizabeth, having been born on a plantation had learned to accept people no matter their position, color or social class. She was friends with the grounds men and she truly respected her nanny and housemaid, Aunt Lucy. Even now she would kill for some of her famous oatmeal porridge and fried dumpling. Her belly growled reminding her it was lunch time.

She met up with Mary and was joined by this handsome white guy Josh, who was in one of her classes. They had quite an interesting interaction, chatting about things they did growing up as children.

Hearing their stories made Liz more appreciative of her own childhood, especially hearing the American talk about how he had one class after another with no time to play with friends. He was never allowed to play outside like a normal child.

She remembered all the awesome things she got to do as child in rural Jamaica. Growing up next to Tafari was her fondest memory. She had watched him build drums, use strings to make guitars, watched as he sang and danced like Bob Marley shaking his locks from side to side. He was a real handyman too. She smiled, hanging her head as she tried to conceal her blush.

She remembered when she would play with her dolls and make pretence Tafari was their dad. Their children were perfect with light chocolate colored skin, which was a combination of their dad's dark chocolate and her caramel. They had their dad's perfect smile and locks that was shoulder length.

He was a super dad too. He helped with their school projects, taught them how to sing and dance and build their own toys from scratch.

Their children also entered festivals as their parents had. There were trophies and medals everywhere. Her smile widened as the perfect imagery gave her peace.

Her lunch companions kept talking about their childhood but Elizabeth was lost in thought of her excellent past and perfect future with the man of her dreams, and the father of her children.

She was brought back to reality when her friend Mary asked, "What's that bright smile all about, daydreaming much?" She looked at Elizabeth expectantly and when an answer wasn't forthcoming, she asked, "Well, who is it?"

"Who is what?" Liz smiled innocently.

"Come on Liz, spill the beans, Josh chipped in. I hope it's me," he smirked. "I couldn't bear thinking of you with another guy."

Liz looked up to see if he was being serious, but he hung his head as if the statement had surprised him too.

She smiled and moved on, "well, it's just a friend I have back home. His name is Tafari."

Her eyes sparkled as she called his name and she could see her friends' interest grow. "He is absolutely perfect. He is tall, dark, with strong arms, firm thighs, and a firm butt."

She covered her mouth as if to recall her last statement, but it was a little late. Mary and Josh looked at her with wide eyes and dropped lips. They had never heard her speak like that before.

Liz had also surprised herself as she had never described anyone so explicitly before, however she couldn't restrain herself. Tafari had that effect on her. "His lips, oh those lips are to die for, his eyes, his marvellous eyes sees way down into my soul, he is pure, seeing only the good in everyone. He is indeed the man of my dreams. Only problem is, my mom hates him."

"So you are in love with this guy?" Josh asked surprised. He never thought for a moment she had a male interest. He had his eyes and heart set on her from the first day she walked into his class.

This may be their first official conversation, but he always admired and knew he wanted her for his girlfriend. He wanted her and he always gets what he wants. Some way or another he would make her forget Mr charming back home.

"Yes, I must say, I am truly in love with him."

"Hmm, sounds like missy has given it up to this Tafari guy," Mary laughed.

"Not that it is any of your business but, I'm still a virgin"

"Wow," Josh thought. That sweetened the deal; not only was she smart and good looking, she was also a virgin. All the girlfriends he had in his past had been passed down through the entire football team before getting to him.

These girls were way too easy. This caramel crunch from the Caribbean was the best fit for his diet and he intended to satisfy his appetite. All this thought about eating made him hungry, his smile was trouble filled as he turned his attention to his lunch.

Another night, another letter. Liz had been writing to Tafari every night since she had been in the US. He had replied to some of her letters, not all. She knew most men didn't love to write, so she appreciated his efforts.
In his letters, he said he was very busy at his new school. He was excited about being at the School of Arts. His programme was Music and Dance, and he was enjoying every minute of it. He explained that he never knew he had it in him to dance so well. He raved about his dance instructor Cherry and how good she was, how flexible, how she reminded him of her. She prayed that it was innocent admiration, as she was aware that admiration was the first step for something romantic to grow.

She promised herself to write to him every night as a constant reminder that she was thinking of him. Tonight she wrote,

My dear Tafari,

Today was no different from any other day, as you were the first thing on my mind when I awoke. At lunch, my friends caught me daydreaming about you. I daydreamed about what our kids will be, their skin complexion and the texture of their hair. I thought about their smile and the type of music they would like to hear. All the trophies they would win from dancing and playing music, and the national competitions they would enter. I eagerly await the day my dreams will come through. Tonight again, I seal this letter with a kiss and always remember, I will always love you.

Elizabeth.

Tafari smiled as he opened yet another letter from Liz. He looked forward to receiving one almost every day. He knew the only reason he didn't receive one on the weekends was because the post office wasn't operational. She always made him smile with her crazy dreams, fond memories, and her new experiences at school. She told him how different it was to studying in Jamaica verses America. He so badly wanted to see America for himself, and hearing about it only heightened his interest.

He would be answering her letter, but he would not let her know his performing group from The School of Arts had been invited to dance at the grand opening of a theatre in the New York within a few weeks. He would be popping in to her school for a surprised visit. He couldn't wait to see her face become burning red with surprise, much as it had the day she realized he was playing at the dance competition in Kingston.

He had already written to his mother to ensure she had enough time to gather Liz's favourite fruits and prepare some of the meals she loved that could take the journey. He knew his mother would be super excited about this as she always worried that Lizzie was not being fed right at the boarding house. Lizzie was her baby, she had cooked almost every meal for her since she was old enough to eat from the family pot. She had written back warning him to keep the visit neutral.

They decided not to say anything about the trip to the Mr and Mrs of the house as they didn't want to give Mrs Blackwood any ideas. Lucy was so proud, her son was going to New York. She knew better days were ahead for him.

Tafari was overly excited and could barely contain himself, he was so tempted to write to Liz, telling her of his trip. He had dreams about her every night since the invite had come. Tafari really felt this would be his opportunity to fulfil the dream he had so many times.

Ever since the night in the tree house he had not forgotten her smell, her delicate touch as she held on to his searching hands, her eager voice as she had told him she needed him. The memory was as fresh as bread from a baker's oven.

She had asked that he keeps himself for her and as difficult as it was, with the temptations he faced at school, he was determined he would. He was indeed a crowd favourite at the dance institute, with girls with all shapes, races and stature wanting to be close to him. Even his dance instructor Cherry had offered to teach him a few things in private, but he always declined with a smile.

He was determined he would hold out for Elizabeth. He knew she was keeping herself for him. She had told him in one of her letters that she had touched herself while thinking about him, and how her panties got wet. She however explained, it didn't feel half as good as that night in the tree house. His male member responded immediately with the memory; he gently reminded his member the wait was almost over.

Elizabeth was feeling extra home sick for the past few days. She had received a letter from her parents saying how badly they missed her. She understood why they would miss her, as she was their only child and they had invested a lot of time and energy into her upbringing over the years, now with her gone, they were bored. Her mom was even toying with the idea of going back to teach.
Tafari too in his letters always said he missed her, and she guessed it was all taking its toll on her.
She woke up today for the first time since being in the States feeling less than enthused about going to school or speaking to anyone. Her roommate had tried to get her attention before she left but she had pulled the sheets a little tighter and pretended not to hear.
She finally decided to drag herself out of bed fifteen minutes before her first class and took all of ten minutes showering, hoping the hot water would revive her. As she crawled out of the bathroom, there was a rushed knock on her bedroom door. She hurriedly opened to see who it was. Her friend Mary was standing there, hands akimbo, staring at her questioningly and scanning the room behind her.

"Why are you knocking down my door as if the building is on fire missy?" Elizabeth smiled to ward off any offence.

"We were worried sick about you."
"We? She peered around the corner to see Josh standing there. "Oh, hi Josh, I see she dragged you along too."
Mary shook her head before answering defensively, "Pardon me for caring. You're always at school an hour before your classes so if you are not there, don't you expect us to check up on you?"
Before Liz could answer Mary pushed past her in the doorway and made her way to Liz's bed.

Josh now stood at the doorway looking her over, and that's when she became conscious she was only wearing a towel with her firm apple breast perking up. Her face turned red with shame, "come on in Josh," she waved a hand.
She grabbed her clothes from the bed and went to the bathroom to get dressed.
"So missy, why are you so late for school?" Mary shouted after her. "We thought you may have been smoking some weed and burnt the place down?"

Mary and Josh laughed but Liz wasn't in the mood for Jamaican jokes.

As a matter of fact, she wasn't in the mood for any jokes, she just wished they would leave but she wasn't about to be rude and ask them to. She stood at the bathroom door looking at them and that's when Mary realized she wasn't sharing in the joke.

"I am not in the frame of mind for school, I just want to go home."

Mary came to stand beside her at the door. She fully understood, as she too was far away from her home country Trinidad. "Ok then, it's final, we are sculling classes today. We will stay here all day, eat, drink, laugh and be merry. Are you in Josh?"

Josh looked at her surprised. He had never been asked to do anything so daring before. He thought about it a few minutes before answering. "Well I can see Liz needs us, so I guess one day won't kill us. Hell yea, I'm in."

"Are you sure about this guys? I really don't wish to put anyone in a compromising position, I'll be fine." She looked at Josh expectantly.

"You are important to me Liz and I want to know that you're ok, so I'm in." He gave her a minute to let it sink in before asking, "So, what are we cooking?"

They all laughed at his boldness before Liz answered, "Ok, I'm going to prepare a real Jamaican dish for the two of you, just relax and let the pro take it from here."

Liz could feel herself relaxing as she gathered the ingredients to prepare curried chicken with white rice for her friends. She had watched Aunt Lucy long enough to know, she got this.

They had a great day together. Mary had changed out of her uniforms and went to a store down the road to get a bottle of Jamaican Appleton with Coke and they drank, ate, sang along to reggae and calypso music, then they slept. It was after six in the evening when they finally parted company. Elizabeth felt alive and ready to take on the world again.

She had to admit, she had not felt this good since getting to the States. Deep down she was still missing home and

Tafari but for tonight, she could sleep well. She knew that summer holidays was five months away and she would be on her way to Jamaica. She would be counting down the days.

Chapter Twelve

The day was finally here for Tafari and his team to travel to the states. The last few weeks were spent in great anticipation. He had gone to bed nightly with pain in his groin as he couldn't get his mind to stop thinking of Elizabeth and the prospects from his trip. He needed Liz and the wait was almost over.

Their flight was at one in the afternoon and they were all busy getting ready. His dance instructor Cherry made multiple visits to his room checking if he was ok, asking if he had everything he needed for the trip and even offered to buy anything he was missing. If only she was aware he had his girlfriend in the States, and thanks to this trip, he was being delivered right into her hands.
He didn't know what his instructor had in mind, but he knew it wouldn't work in her favor, as he was going to make Elizabeth Blackwood into a woman. She was going to be all his. He smiled mischievously at the thought.

The bus came at eleven to take them to the Airport. They were all very excited. Except for the instructors, they were all travelling for the first time.

At the airport, the check-in was pretty smooth and before long they had boarded their flight. They were in business class but that was ok, as they all got a chance to sit together. The party comprised of ten dancers and two instructors. Juan, who was the deputy instructor said a powerful prayer before take-off. They played games and sang old gospel songs until they finally landed at the JFK Airport in New York. It was late in the evening so Tafari decided to rest and visit Elizabeth the next day. He would have to take a bus to get to her school which would be a little nerve racking as he never had to travel alone in such a gigantic city before. This place was almost as large as the entire Jamaica, but he was too excited to care. He couldn't wait to see her.

Since the day they had decided not to show up for classes, Elizabeth and Josh had been spending a lot of time together. They spent many evenings studying as they had a few classes together. He would come to her dorm after classes and they would study until they were both tired. He was really fun to be around. Sometimes she thought she saw a hint of a crush, but then he would just laugh whenever she asked him why he was staring or why he had held on to her hands for an extended time.

She could see why he or any guy would have a crush on her as she had become a really desirable woman. She couldn't walk around school without multiple guys trying to get her attention. Pity they didn't know their tries were in vain as the only man she was interested in was Tafari. Even now she wished he was here.

Tonight they were studying Psychology. It wasn't her favourite subject, but Josh was really good at it, and she wasn't about to fail a subject so she asked for his help. He was also pursuing a Bachelor's of Science so they saw a lot of each other. They even had lunch together most times. Mary wasn't always available to join them as she was studying Journalism and that meant her class schedule was different. Elizabeth mostly saw her at dance classes as they both had the same minor.

At about ten, Elizabeth announced that it was time for bed and walked Josh to the door. As they said good night and he was about to walk away, she thought she heard him say, "I love you Elizabeth."

She sought clarity as it wasn't clear, "Did you say something Josh?"

"Yes, I said, Good night Elizabeth."

Elizabeth smiled as she watched him walk away. She knew what she had heard, but she also knew she couldn't entertain it as that would mean setting up an innocent young man to have his heart broken. Her heart was taken. It belonged to Tafari.

Today was the day, Tafari woke up pretty early. His team went through their dance routine to ensure they had it down, as they had one day to go until performances. He had already advised his trainers that he would be spending the night with family. He gave Cherry an address belonging to his Father's brother which she verified to be valid before granting him permission. This was the rule established before leaving Jamaica.

After rehearsal, everyone had lunch. Tafari then went back to his hotel room and ran a warm bath. He rid his body of all unwanted hair then soaked in the masculine fragrant body wash given to him by Cherry before they left for the trip. His mother had a Taylor made black suit done for him as she thought he may need it to go out for a celebratory party with his team after their performance. He however decided to wear it for Elizabeth. After all, she had not seen him in months; she was sure to appreciate him in a suit.

He accessorized it with a cream long sleeve shirt and decided to leave the top button undone so it would reveal his curly, black chest hair. His seams were so sharp they threatened to cut. His hair was done up in an elastic band and fell comfortable on his shoulder. He moisturized his lips and looked himself over in the mirror. "Quite dapper, if I may say so myself," he laughed at the over-confidence he was exhibiting, ignoring the jitters in his stomach.

It was now half past three, Tafari headed off to the bus station with the directions he had been given by his mom, and all the sweetness of home. Liz would be ecstatic to see him as he had everything she loved dearly, mangoes, roasted breadfruit, fried fish, pudding and himself of course. He was overly excited and couldn't wait to see her face lit up. He imagined she would hurl herself at him, much as she had that day she was released from the hospital.

He wasn't going to rush. He had all intention of spending the night on her dorm. He would let her call the shots. Tonight she was master and he, her noble servant. Truth be told, he already knew how tonight would turn out, as she wanted him just as much as he wanted her.

The bus ride from New York to Pennsylvania was about two hours but it would be worth it. He brought along his walk man and cassettes so he could listen some music on his way. He was told that the white Americans could be very unfriendly and may not want to offer him a seat. The bus he boarded had mostly Blacks, so he easily found the perfect window seat where he could enjoy the view.

It was a long but breath-taking drive. He had never seen buildings that tall before. Everything looked so different from home. He could see that the people living in these areas he passed were rich folks. There were no small houses in view.

He wondered what it would be like to live in a house like that, and what they had for dinner. He bet it wasn't yams, green banana, dumplings and salted mackerel, as was found on their table back home most evenings. They must have turkey all the time. He sighed and turned his attention to his walk-man instead.

It was a gift from his dance instructor. She told him it was very expensive as it was pretty new on the market. She emphasized that she only gave gifts to people she cared about. She praised him for being a great dancer and the face of the group.

He must give her credit, she was trying pretty hard. He however knew he couldn't let her in, as his heart was not his to give.

At six, he arrived at the University. He gave the security a letter that was drafted by and signed his mother granting him permission to see Elizabeth. The security took quite a few minutes to verify that Lucy was listed as a next of kin before finally allowing him in.

As he walked up the stairs, excitement mixed with fear, he read and followed the directions given to him by the security. She was on the third floor, room number twenty-six. He completed the final staircase and realized the first door was number twenty one. There were six rooms, so he estimated that her door would be the final one in the passage.

He had passed a few persons on the stairwell that gave him a stare, but for the most part the dorm was quiet. He decided to wait one to two minutes allowing his nerves to be settled before going to her door. He was startled by a female voice coming up behind him.

"Hi my name is Stacy. You are a cute one." She smiled at him flirtatiously before continuing, "Why haven't I seen you around here before?"

He looked around to ensure that she was actually talking to him before he responded with a smile. "Actually, I don't go to school here. My name is Tafari, I'm just visiting a friend."

"Tafari?" She thought about the name for a minute. "Where have I heard that name before? Where are you from Tafari?"

"I'm from Jamaica."

"OMG, Liz's Tafari! Are you here to see Elizabeth Blackwood?"

"As a matter of fact, I am."

Liz spoke about him every day. It was impossible for Stacy not to recognize his name. This young man was way more attractive than Liz had revealed, as a matter of fact, he was drop dead gorg.

"Come with me, I'll take you to her. She's my roommate. I bet she doesn't know you're coming because she would have said so. She's going to die when she sees you. I'm going to enjoy watching her turn red."

Stacy laughed then gestured for him to follow her.

Chapter Thirteen

Liz and Josh had met up at six for yet another study session on Psychology, as Liz still needed some clarity on a paper they were given to present on. He was pointing to something in his book and Liz leaned forward for a closer look when their hands brushed. She looked up with the intention to apologize but was greeted by warm lips. Stunned by his sudden boldness, she couldn't move, and he took the opportunity to explore her lips.

Liz didn't hear the door open. Stacy cleared her throat to get their attention and that's when Liz realized two figures were standing there in the shadow. One, she easily made out to be her roommate and the other was a gentleman wearing a suit. She couldn't see his face, but she could tell he was stunning. As his face came into perspective, she realized it was Tafari.

Tafari is here. She wondered if it was all a bad dream and if she would wake up any minute now. Was Tafari really in the United States? Liz was filled with excitement, but that quickly turned to panic as she realized the position she had been caught in. Josh couldn't have picked a worst time to express himself. He had so many opportunities before today and couldn't find the courage, why now? Why when Tafari had come to surprise her? Her eyes welled up with tears. What was she going to say? What could she really say?

Panic crippled her movement. She could only sit there and stare at him. She wanted to run to him, but how could she explain her present position? Would he believe if she told him it had not happened before? After all, she wasn't fighting Josh when they walked in.

Tafari had not uttered a word all this time, he just stood there looking at her through pain filled eyes. The bags he was carrying had become loose and a mango fell to the ground and rolled to her feet. Her heart broke even more when she realized he had brought her favourite fruit. He had everything she wanted. Tears streamed down her face.

She had to say something, anything, he just had to forgive her for this err. She got up and moved in his direction, hoping she could hug him. She prayed she could make him see that the kiss was not intentional, and she would get the chance to explain that Josh was just a study partner.

Tafari stood there motionless, watching her approach, and as if he could no longer control it, tears started running freely like a river overflowing its banks. He leaned against a nearby wall for support. She could see his heart break as he continued to look at her distraught.

Oh God, She never meant to hurt him, she had to say something to make this right. She had made him a promise, and had kept herself for him all these years, it couldn't end like this. She was crushed seeing him cry. She held a hand up to wipe his eyes, but he turned away sharply.

Tafari could not believe this. This was the last thing he could have expected. How could anyone be so deceptive? Was this the same girl who wrote to him every day telling him how badly she missed him? He remembered his mom had told him of the events that unfolded between Uncle John and her parents when she was admitted to the hospital, he guessed deception was in her blood. She told him she loved him and she knew he loved her, and now this. How could Liz have found a lover in America? And not just any lover, he was white. That reality hit home like Muhammad Alli at a million dollar fight. His tears started flowing again. He bet this guy was also studying Medicine too; someone she could be proud to take home to her family. He bet her parents would be proud of her now. The thought made him want to drop everything and leave; forgetting all about this lying, deceptive slut who took his heart and crushed it beneath her feet.

He was never going to forgive her for this. How would he ever trust another woman who said she loved him? His tears flowed loosely as he reflected on the demise of the beautiful future he had planned with this girl.

The silence was deafening. Elizabeth had to say something, even though his face was as hard as bricks, she had to try. "I am so very sorry Tafari. This has never happened before, you must believe me. He is only a study partner."

She glanced in Josh's direction before continuing, "we have been studying together for a while and I guess he has become fond of me. He got a little carried away and kissed me, but I wasn't kissing back, I promise you." She turned around to face Josh. "Tell him Josh, please tell him this was the first time." She tried to hold on to Tafari who pulled his hand away.

Josh thought for a moment about what Liz was asking him to do. Truth is, he was in love with this girl. He never had anyone in his life who made him feel more alive. He could easily see himself coming home to her warm smile and her Jamaican cuisine every evening. She may hate him for the while when her relationship with this dread is over, but he would be there to help her pick up the pieces. He knew he could help her heal and in the process, she would fall in love with him, she had to.

Was he supposed to agree to this and just allow her to dismiss his feelings? There was no way he could let that happen. He turned around to face Tafari. "Actually Elizabeth is my girlfriend and I love her." Stacy who had been quiet all this time gave Liz a dirty look, as if to say, 'girl, you have two men.' Without even saying it, Liz knew she was being judged, she however had nothing to prove to Stacy. She just couldn't allow Tafari to leave with the perception that she had deceived him.

"As a matter of fact," Josh continued, "I think you're harassing her and I'm going to get the security to escort you off the property."

With this he was out the door with Elizabeth following swiftly behind him. "No Josh, no! You've always heard me talk about Tafari. How could you do this to me? I hate you. We will never be friends after this. I hate you."

Tafari stepped out of the room and strolled past them arguing. "You don't need to get the security, I'll escort myself out."

He paused to look Elizabeth directly in the eyes. "I must tell you Lizzie, you have really hurt me. I don't know how I am going to get over this, but one thing's for sure, I will, because there are no powers that could get me to forgive you.

She opened her mouth to try convincing him that she would never hurt him, but it was too late, he had already become a shadow down the hallway.

She couldn't move. Her knees gave way, and before she knew it, she was on the ground. Liz couldn't stop crying, his name the only word she could say.
Josh attempted to lift her but her look was like venom when she realized it was him. He knew he was the last person she wanted to see right now.

Stacy who had been a bystander watching the events unfold waved a hand for him to go. She knelt down to comfort her room-mate, she wasn't going to judge, as what Liz needed was a friend. She could see these events had brought her great pain.

Chapter Fourteen

The two hours drive back to the hotel was torture for Tafari as he could not get the horrid image out of his mind. He replayed the kiss a hundred times over. If she wasn't into it, why didn't she pull away or slap his face? She said she wasn't kissing back, but she certainly wasn't stopping him. How could she allow another man to touch her after she begged him to keep himself for her, after she promised to keep herself for him?

She had written to him every day with this promise and tonight when the time was right, she had betrayed him. His body had been so excited at the thought of finally discovering her hidden treasures.

Over the past few months, since being in college, so many temptations had come his way, but he had held on, all in anticipation of the day he would finally have her. Now what? His body was ready. He had sleepless nights, waking with his male member wet from dreams about her. His body needed her, but now that she wasn't an option, his body needed someone.

By the time he got back to the hotel it was almost twelve. He quietly entered his room, ran a hot shower, soaking from head to toes, all in an effort to get his mind to forget the events of the evening. He thought about Cherry, but quickly shunned the feeling as he didn't relish the idea of using a woman just to fulfil his sexual thirst. After all, he would never want a man to do that to one of his sisters. Cherry was quite a fine woman. She possessed the shape of a coke bottle, firm breast, small waist, nice sturdy legs, an excellent dance instructor and the best part was, she was interested in him. He however wouldn't encourage her interest, as he knew he wasn't in love with her.

He couldn't however stop his body from responding positively to the thought of her. He was instantly hard the minute she popped into his head. "Oh shit, Tafari, you have to control yourself," he talked himself down quietly.

The last thing he wanted was to make a rash decisions that would have an adverse effect on his future. He tried desperately to regain control of his thoughts. As the water ran over his body, he began to free his mind of all thoughts, and eventually his erection subsided. He decided to spend a few more minutes in the shower, then it would be time for bed.

A squeak at the door caught his attention. He turned off the shower and stood there silently, listening, trying to confirm if someone was in his room, or if he was hallucinating. "Tafari" the soft sweet voice pierced the silence. He peeked out from behind the shower curtain to find Cherry standing there with a concerned look on her face.

"You weren't supposed to be back until tomorrow, so when I saw your lights on, I got worried. I knocked and when you didn't respond, I got the front desk to let me in. Is everything ok?"

"I…um, he stuttered, becoming conscious that he was naked and Cherry was standing in his bathroom. "I'm really not sure how to answer you. I would love to say yes, be the man my mother brought me up to be, but truth is, I am confused."

"Do you want to talk about it?"
His eyes became blurred with tears. "No, I don't."

"It is very important not to keep things bottled up inside Tafari. It will eat away at your soul." She searched his face, trying to understand his emotional state. "Remember, I am not just your trainer, I am also your friend. She walked closer to the shower. Her tone lowered to a whisper, "As a matter of fact, I think I'm in love with you."

"That's what she said too, and then I find her kissing another man." The tears started flowing now. "How could she have loved me and hurt me so badly?"
She realized then that the trip he made earlier was to visit a girl and not family as he had communicated. That was pretty clever of him.
She was sad to see him hurting. A sweet young gentleman like himself, deserved to be loved and appreciated. She felt a sudden urge to hold him, hoping he would feel her love, words alone could not express how she felt, nor provide him with the comfort he needed tonight.
Tafari watched as she rid her body of her robe and panties. He didn't try to stop her, as even if his lips had said no, his body had already betrayed his thoughts.
"Tafari," Cherry broke the silence, her tone, very comforting. "I understand your pain, as this girl was obviously your first love, but I can show you what it really means to be loved. I can help you heal."
She brushed her hand against his cheek, "I too have been through a heart-break. I know exactly how you are feeling."
She looked into his eyes for a connection. "You feel all

women are the same; you wonder how you will ever trust again. You need to realize that she wasn't right for you, just as, he wasn't right for me. The sooner you let her go, the sooner you will see that what you are looking for is right here." She took his hand and directed it to her face.

She climbed into the shower and squeezed some of his shower gel into her hands. She rubbed his shoulders hoping that would help him to relax. Before long, she could feel some of the tension ease and his tears dried. This encouraged her to take things a step further. She opened his hands and placed some of the liquid into it, then directed them to her firmly erected breasts.

He responded like a child gripping its mother's breast for the first time. She enjoyed every minute of his eager, slightly aggressive touch. She wondered if this would be his first time, but decided it wouldn't be the right time to ask. If it was, she would find out eventually. She hoped that was the case, as she would enjoy grooming him into her dream lover.

She held on to his cheek and guided his lips to her own before whispering, "This will be our little secret, ok." She planted a long warm kiss on his lips while guiding his hand to the heat between her thighs.

He found a soft spot and began to rub in a circular motion. She lost herself to this feeling and before long, she moaned with pleasure, as she came.

That brought her excitement to peek, and she decided, she wasn't about to stop now, she wanted to feel all of him. Though her initial intention was just to comfort him, keeping things neutral was no longer an option.

Cherry smiled as their heads finally hit the pillow that night, fully satisfied how well he had followed her instructions.

The sheets were rooted from the bed and now laid tangled on the floor as evidence of their wild love making that had lasted for over an hour.

He had lifted her from the bath and taken her to the bed as she begged for more, and boy did she receive more. She came to the conclusion that it could not have been his first experience as there was no way he could be so damn good if he wasn't taught. She wished she had gotten the chance to train him in that area too, however he was so good, she could not complain. So much better than a good meal and fine wine, she reflected.

Tafari awoke in Cherry's arms very early the next morning. Her afterglow was brilliant, like sunshine on fresh spring water. It made him want to take her again. He would enjoy having her scream like she had the night before.

His skin still burnt from the impression left behind by her nails, as she had lost control and gripped him all five times she came. There was no way she could tell that was his first experience because he had applied all he had learnt from years of reading playboy magazines. He rolled over for a kiss but she placed a finger on his lips and whispered, "Very soon my eager one, very soon, I promise." She got up, got dressed, and left. He figured she didn't want to risk being seen by the other group members who would be getting up early to practice.

At six in the evening, they all left the hotel for the theatre. Cherry sat beside Tafari and chit-chatted with him the entire way. Just before going in, she encouraged him to leave an expression on the audience, and that he did. She had never seen him perform so passionately. She smiled as she remembered last night and decided his performance tonight must be as a result of that.

The crowd seemed to be in full agreement, as everyone in the auditorium gave a standing ovation when the group's performance was over.

When they entered backstage, cameras were waiting and after taking multiple pictures, a gentleman who was waiting approached Tafari and asked to speak to him for a few minutes.

"Young man, I must tell you, I have never seen such a stellar performance in all my years of watching and teaching dance."

Tafari shuck his head, feeling honoured. "Thank you sir"

"Pardon my manners, my name is Señor John Michael, A Professor at the most credited school of the arts anywhere in the United States. Without any shadow of a doubt young sir, our degree program in Performing Arts would be honoured to have someone like you."

Tafari looked at him in awe. He always thought of himself as being a good dancer, but never thought he was that good. The gentleman continued, "A full scholarship awaits you, tuition and boarding paid. We also have a dance group that performs at events such as this, you can join and make extra income. If you do decide, we would love to have you."

Tafari thought about it for a minute. He wasn't one to make hasty decisions as his mom always warned him about impulsive behaviour and the implications they could have on his life.

"Do you have an address where I can write to you sir? I will have to discuss this with my parents and get back to you." He would be leaving for Jamaica in two days. He would speak to his parents then and get word back.

"Oh sure son, there's no rush, you do have a few months to decide. After all, the new school term doesn't begin for the next seven months." He wrote the address and gave this to Tafari, "I look forward to hearing from you." They nodded in agreement then the professor walked away.

Tafari couldn't believe his fortune. This could be his big opportunity to make his parents proud. He figured they would be caught between excitement and fear, as he was their last child and the closest one to them. He knew mothers especially, found it difficult to let go off their last child, but he was sure they would want him to take up this opportunity. He just needed to confirm out of respect and love for them.

The next two days they spent in the US was used for sight-seeing and shopping. Tafari was from a more humble background than most of the others and didn't have much to spend. The rest of the team however was not aware, as he was spoiled rotten by Cherry.

She bought him everything his little heart desired, even tokens to take back as gifts for his parents. They were spending a lot of time together and he was becoming very fond of her.

Since the night they had spent together, she had not returned to his room. He figured this was because she didn't wish to compromise her position and lose the respect of the team.

He could still feel the effects of her in his groin. Her memory was fresh in his mind, and her essence left behind on his pillow haunted him at nights. Even now, he had an immediate reaction to her memory. He quickly changed his thoughts as he was out with the entire team having lunch and did not care for the embarrassment. He wanted more of her for sure and once they were back in Jamaica, he was going to have her.

Even though he had such a good connection with Cherry, he could not get his mind to stop thinking about Elizabeth. He thought about her daily. He wondered if she was longing for him, or if she was being comforted by that white guy. He couldn't get her voice out of his head as she had streamed his name again and again that night when he had walked away.

Was she just being an actress, after realizing the position she had been caught in, or was it genuine? Was she really hurting? Was that guy really forcing himself on her? Before the deception, he had believed she loved him, but now, he didn't know what to believe. What was however clear was, it was too late for them. She had really hurt him, and he had moved on.

He knew his mother would be expecting a feedback on his visit. He would have to tell her a story as the truth just would not do.

Chapter Fifteen

Back in Jamaica, he spent a day at school, after which, he went to visit his parents in St Elizabeth, taking along the gifts bought by Cherry.

His mother ran out to meet him as she was pretty excited with his return.

He gave her a lovely story of Elizabeth and how well she was doing, how she spoke of her and was very excited about the packages she sent.

He went to check that all was well in his tree house before walking the grounds and greeting everyone, including the Blackwoods. He wished he could tell them he had seen their daughter, but he had promised his mom he wouldn't.

When his dad came home, they had dinner as a family. It felt just like old times. After the kitchen was cleared, his mom asked to speak with him privately. When they were settled on the veranda chair, she held on to his hands, "son that was a good story you presented about Elizabeth. If I didn't receive a letter from her yesterday, you would have had me fooled." His mother searched his face for a reaction to her revelation. She wanted to approach this with due care as, if her son was hurting, she would never wish to compound his pain. She knew how he felt about Elizabeth and from the details in her letter, she knew he must be torn.

When she didn't see any sign of emotion, she proceeded cautiously. "Elizabeth explained in her letter that the encounter with the young man had never happened before. My son, knowing this girl like I do, seeing that I practically raised her from a babe, I am leaning towards believing her."

She wished she could tell what he was feeling as he still held a straight face with no sign of emotion. She knew he was strong, as that was the way she grew him, however she felt he was trying hard to put up a front in this case.

She thought about what she was going to say a moment longer before she spoke again, "I know I didn't encourage a relationship between you two, and I have always encouraged you to stay in your lane, but I have been around long enough to know true love when I see it, and son, that girl is in love with you."

"Mom, I really don't know how she could do this to me." He started on a higher pitch than intended. He quickly corrected his tone then continued, "I was so in love with her and I don't know if I want to forgive her for allowing another man to touch her in that way."

"She is begging for your forgiveness son. I believe you should at least give her a chance to explain. After all, I don't believe there is anything she could say to hurt you more" She let out a breath, "son, I would normally warn you to stay away from Elizabeth because of her parents, but I believe it would be a real shame to see something so rich, a love so strong wither and die." She touched his face to offer comfort.

She spent a few more minutes appealing to her son to talk to Lizzie and to reiterate what the bible said about forgiveness. She knew this was conflicting as she had always asked him to stay his route, but to hell with what should be, love breaks all barriers.

"On the topic of opportunity mother, I have great news. I have been offered a full scholarship to study music and dance at one of the most prestigious universities in the United States." His moms face brightened like sunshine making its way over a mountain top. He went on, "Tuition and boarding fully paid. This could be my chance to make it to the big times mom," he added excitingly.

Lucille got up and ran into the house without saying a word to her son. A few minutes later, she emerged with his dad. She couldn't stop screaming from excitement but Marcus was able to keep his composure. He told his son how proud he was of him and encouraged him not to miss this opportunity as it sometimes came once in a lifetime.

Lucy was however over the top with excitement, so much so that her eyes filled with tears. Her son was going to University in The United States of America. She thought she would burst with pride. "This is wonderful news my baby." She held on to his face and kissed his cheek.

His father too gave him a hug. He had never really been hugged by his dad before. He always knew his dad loved him, but Marcus wasn't one to show emotions. This made him even more excited about accepting the offer made by Mr Michael. He would write to him as soon as he returned to school.

The weekend was over and Tafari was back in school. He wasn't surprised to see two letters awaiting him from Elizabeth. She repeated all the things his mother had told him and begged his forgiveness. She said she had not eaten a wholesome meal since he left, as she did not know what she would do if he didn't love her anymore.

He thought about it for a few days, reflecting on what his mom had said about knowing her as well as she did, and reading the letters again and again, until finally, he decided to reply. He told her that he had forgiven her and that he could see this was truly a mistake. He also apologized for the pain she had suffered since the encounter. He asked her to be comforted and assured her they would get pass it.
He also told her about the scholarship he was offered, and that he would be accepting and moving to New York in a matter of months. He did not mention what had happened between himself and Cherry as he knew she would be devastated. He would always cherish the memories he made with Cherry, but he was going to be with his true love.

Now all he needed to do was to break off his friendship with Cherry. She was a big girl. She would be alright. After all, she had the type of body a man would kill to possess. A good-looking career woman with a killer shape, bright smile, a go-getter personally, and most importantly, she was willing to spoil her man. No man could resist that.

Since coming back to school he couldn't quite put his fingers on it but there was something strange about Cherry's behaviour. She was missing from dance classes a lot. This is something she had never done before, and when she was there, she wasn't the energetic, vibe master he knew her to be.

He wondered if she had returned sick from their trip but when he asked, she assured him she was ok. She told the team that she just needed rest. She went to the doctor and was given a sick leave for the next two weeks. He would miss having her around.

Before she left, she had arranged for them to have a date the following Saturday. He would meet her for dinner and then go to see a movie. He decided that would be his chance to break things off gently. The thought of likely hurting a woman who didn't deserve it, really broke his heart.

He found it hard to sleep the nights leading up to their date as he continued to struggle with the thought that she may be hurt by his decision. A woman like her deserved to be cherished.

The week ran off so quickly. Tafari and Cherry met in the town and walked to the movie theatre together. After the movie they had dinner at a hotel she had booked for them to spend the night.

They had a few drinks at the bar. She only had soft drinks which was unlike her, but he figured she may be on meds since she had gone to see the doctor. She was however as energetic as before, laughing and chatting with the hotel staff. Even encouraging a flirt here and there. He was glad to see her being herself again. His emotions were mixed as he knew what he was about to do, and he did not know how she would take it.

At about eleven, they decided to retire for the evening. He watched her from behind as she walked ahead of him to the room. She seemed a lot better than she had going off on sick leave. She looked well rested and even seemed to have put on a few pounds. She was a striking beauty in a tall floral dress that swept her feet as she moved.

The colors complimented her dark skin completely. He hoped she would handle his decision the way she handled everything else, with grace.

As they entered the room Tafari began, "thank you for a great evening. I don't deserve any of this, I don't deserve...."

His words were stolen by Cherry's hungry assault on his lips. Her tongue found its way into his mouth and desperately searched for his, and when she had found it, she entwined her own around it, sucking gently, enjoying herself.

"You taste so good," she whispered. "I've missed you Tafari. Didn't you miss me? I'm surprised you came here to talk." She laughed, pushing him against the wall before continuing her assault.

His mind said stop, but he had lost all will to move. She really knew how to touch a man and let him lose his senses. He held on to her shoulders as his knees became too weak to hold him. After about three minutes of French kissing, he finally regained his consciousness and held on to her hands which were now desperately trying to loosen his belt buckle. "Stop, we need to talk".

"And you can't tell me after we were through?" She tried again to move in with an eager thrust, but he pulled further away.

"No, I cannot. After you hear what I have to say, you may never want to see me again."

She looked at him wide eyed and sat sullenly on the bed, then snapped, "go ahead."

He sat beside her and took her hand. He wanted her to be as calm as possible. He really had no intention to hurt her.

"You see Cherry, when we were in New York, after the performance, a gentleman from a renowned School of Arts approached and offered me a full scholarship, room and board included. After discussions with my parents, I have decided to take up his offer."
"But we can still be together even if you're in the United States, after all, I hold a US Visa. I perform at lots of shows in the US."

She hoped he wasn't saying all this to say that he was contemplating a break-up as she was already in too deep, and was not willing to let him go.
"There is more," he sighed. "Remember I told you I had walked in on my girlfriend with a white guy? It turns out he had forced himself on her. She was distraught and begged me to forgive her, and I have finally decided to."
He used his hands to cover his face, "I guess what I am saying is, what we have been doing cannot continue as I am in love with Elizabeth and I am going to be with her." He shook his head in regret and refused to look her in the eyes. He didn't know if she would cry but her tears were the last thing he wanted to see. He just could not imagine breaking another woman's heart. Even now, he still remembered Elizabeth's cry of anguish that night when he walked away. He wasn't sure what he would do if Cherry started crying.
When he finally made eye contact, she was sitting there with the kind of look in her eyes that he was afraid of, she was hurt. She was really hurt.
As tears started flowing down her cheeks, he could feel his own eyes burning. He never imagined she would be this hurt, after all, it was just an insignificant fling that lasted a

few weeks. At least that's what he thought. He realized now that it had meant way more than that to her.

He knew one couldn't foretell what would happen when it came to matters of the heart, but he was really hoping she was strong enough not to cry. She would get over him, he knew that. She would have learnt from her first heartbreak to protect her heart from pain. She was too good of a catch to wallow in sadness over him. She could get any man she desired to replace him in a jiffy.

He wondered if she realized how powerful she was. He couldn't understand why she cried.

He placed his hand on her cheek and wiped away the teardrops that were flowing down. "I really didn't mean to hurt you. I know you care about me because care is all you have shown over the past few months. You're the type of woman any man would want and if I hadn't known Elizabeth all my life, I would have never considered giving up on us."

 He held on to her chin, lifting her head, looking into her tear filled eyes as he continued. "You are the perfect catch. You are not just a pretty face, you are intelligent, sexy, talented and best of all, you show a man what it means to be cared for. What man could resist that?"

She still sat there staring down at her hands, teardrops flowing, reflecting on his last question. He was a man, and he could obviously resist her, as he was ready to run off to his college girlfriend in the states not caring if his actions would hurt her. The time they spent together may have been short, but it was certainly enough for her to fall in love. She thought she had learnt to protect herself from a broken heart, but now she realized, the walls around her heart had been shattered the moment she laid eyes on Tafari Messiah.

He wished she would say something. A scream, a push, or a punch on his chest with rolled fist would have let him know what she was thinking. At least then he would know what to say to offer some amount of comfort.
After a few more minutes of subbing, she finally spoke in a low pitch. "Well Tafari, It's a little too late for running off to your college girlfriend."

He heard her speak but her words came in bits and pieces because of the tears. "I'm sorry Cherry, I couldn't hear you. Can you please repeat?"
This time she held her head up and looked at him unwavering, "It's a little too late for your decision to go running off to your perfect little princess, because I'm pregnant."

See what happens next in part two of this three part series.

Will Tafari stand and take responsibility?

Will he run off to New York and never look back?

Will he have his happily ever after with Elizabeth?

You must tune in to find out....see you 2020......

ABOUT YOUR AUTHOR

I am an enthusiast for writing and have been writing poetry as a hobby since age fifteen.
I enjoy seeing the characters come to life and being able to control the outcome. I currently have two published pieces,
"Poetry from a Jamaican Soul" and my latest work 'Rasta Love.'
I decided to venture into Romance because, I am a sucker for a good love story and believe everyone deserves to find their
'happily ever after.'
I am a Wife, a Mother of two Champion boys, a Stepmother, a Student, a Customer Service Professional, an Assistant Youth Fellowship Director, but most importantly, I am a God-fearing Christian woman. Writing is a hobby that I intend to nurture until it blossoms into a fruitful career.

I truly believe music and poetry are two art forms that expresses a message from the soul and that they help to heal both the author and reader/listener.
I look forward to a long and lasting relationship as writer and fan:-)
Thank you

A big thank you to all those who helped my dream become a reality. Those who gave encouragement, guidance and creative ideas.

Special thanks to Ms. Sandrene Mcghie who guided my hands through the editing process.

Thanks to God Almighty for knowledge, creativity and strength.

www.ingramcontent.com/pod-product-compliance
Lightning Source LLC
Chambersburg PA
CBHW071207130726
47998CB00002B/658